"You'll have to control your attraction to me if we're going to work together. Now let me go."

He couldn't obey her. He liked holding her close. It was the only way he could be certain that she felt as he did. She could not put on her ice-princess act when she was in his arms. He saw Mariella's beauty up close. Her smooth skin had felt warm and soft beneath his kiss. And the brilliance of her large black-brown eyes and silken lashes came through. She was more than beautiful, she was delicious. Like a French pastry—exquisite to look at and even better to taste.

"Are you finished?"

"Almost," he said as he kissed her forehead then released her. "I'll control myself, but can you do the same?"

DARA GIRARD's

love of stories started with listening to the imaginative tales of her immigrant parents and grandparents. At age twelve, she sent out her first manuscript. After thirteen years of rejection, she got a contract. She started writing romance because she loves the "dance" between two people falling in love. She is the author of *Table for Two, Gaining Interest, Carefree, Illusive Flame, The Sapphire Pendant* and *Sparks*. Her novels are known for their humor, interesting plot twists and witty dialogue. Dara lives in Maryland. Visit her Web site, www.daragirard.com, or write to her at P.O. Box 10345, Silver Spring, MD 20914.

DARA GIRARD

Taming MARIELLA

KIMANI™ ROMANCE

KIMANI PRESS™

ISBN-13: 978-0-373-86050-0
ISBN-10:   0-373-86050-1

TAMING MARIELLA

www.kimanipress.com

Printed in U.S.A.

Dear Reader,

I knew I wanted to write a story about another Duvall
sister from *The Glass Slipper Project* and my first choice
was sweet Daniella. However, the eldest, Mariella,
demanded center stage, and she was a challenge I couldn't
resist. How could I match this spoiled, opinionated, vain
and stubborn woman who thought of love as impractical,
with her perfect counterpart?

Fortunately, my solution came in the form of a wealthy,
arrogant man named Ian Cooper, who had little interest
in models—ex or otherwise—but who had a dilemma.
He needed Mariella to fulfill his father's will. As these two
embarked on a classic war of the sexes, love emerged. I
hope you enjoy their story.

If you'd like to hear more about my other books or sign
up on my mailing list, please visit my Web site,
www.daragirard.com, or write me at P.O. Box 10345,
Silver Spring, MD 20914.

Sincerely,

Dara Girard

Chapter 1

"He's late." The tall attractive woman looked at her assistant with growing annoyance. Her brilliant brown eyes, surrounded by impossibly long lashes, surveyed the chaos around her. Her expression was serene, just like the face that had graced the cover of top magazines, and for the past three years, had been associated with Desire perfume. Her long dark hair was pulled back in a ponytail capped by a white pinwheel hat while large dangling gold hoop earrings hung from her ears, nearly reaching her shoulders.

"I'm sure he'll be here soon," her assistant, Gen Moser, replied. She looked at Mariella through

almond-shaped brown eyes she had inherited from
her Japanese mother while a rosy shade of pink
touched her honey-colored skin reflecting her
Ghanaian father's ancestry. Her exotic features had
been all the rage years ago, but that hadn't lasted.
She wore her wavy dark hair piled high, held in
place with a finely decorated hair comb. A fitted
blue silk blouse draped her tall, slender frame complemented by low-waist straight-leg jeans. Gen kept
her voice soft, knowing that was the best way to
handle Mariella when she was in one of her
"moods."

Mariella rubbed the back of her neck trying to
ease the tension gathering there. "*Soon* is not soon
enough." She stifled a need to scream. She hated
when things didn't go her way, but was very
careful not to let that show. Mariella Duvall
always looked ready for a camera. That was her
trademark.

She had a long elegant neck that had been
graced with diamonds and emeralds, dark flashing
eyes that had tempted women to buy eyeliner and
mascara; skin like polished oak that looked touch-
ably soft, even in a flat two-dimensional form.
She moved quickly but as gracefully as a trained
dancer, reflecting the years of dance lessons her
parents had paid for. Unfortunately, she'd grown
too tall to make dance her profession.

At all times, Mariella was careful to censor the

type of expressions she allowed to cross her face. Right now a slight pursing of her lips displayed a mild irritation though her words had been spoken with a quiet anger that made her assistant cast an anxious sideward glance at her and inwardly tremble.

This delay was not in the budget or the schedule. She had planned everything to perfection—down to the last detail, and now this! She and Gen had searched days for the perfect location for an important photography assignment. Her choice hadn't failed her. The summer day had brought cloudless skies and an even temperature of eighty degrees. A pristine blue sky embraced the manicured green grass of Woodland Park Botanical Gardens. The location was surrounded by tall birch and maple trees with a small brook that flowed under a stone bridge. Within the immediate enclosure, a gazebo sat serenely surrounded by an assortment of exotic and unusual plants and flowers. It was perfect.

In contrast, the shoot was anything but. Three gorgeous leggy models, dressed in wool coats and mufflers surrounded by fake snow, continued to loudly voice their complaints. The heat was getting to them, and they wanted to get on with the shoot. Damn, if the male model didn't show up, the shoot would be a bust and she'd have to re-schedule. She knew her client, Bretton, wouldn't pay for additional time. Besides, she needed to get the shoot done today, in time for their winter issue.

For a moment, Mariella thought she probably shouldn't have taken the job. She should have just stayed with taking pictures of celebrities. That was what she was good at. But the Bretton shoot was an opportunity to expand her portfolio and put money in the bank, and in addition, get her work seen by new clientele. Messing this up would set her career back years. She'd fought to get the job. She took a deep breath and walked a few feet away from the scene assuring herself that this wouldn't be a catastrophe.

"Isn't that Mariella Duvall?" she heard a woman a few feet away whisper. She didn't turn her head, but out of the corner of her eye saw two women. One wore hot pink spandex and a sports bra and the other woman wore an overly large blue T-shirt sporting an enormous college logo across the front. Mariella was used to people whispering about her. In school they'd whispered about her being a snob. In college they'd whispered about her being dumb. After college they'd whispered about her parents' deaths and her family's financial difficulties. When she'd reached New York they'd whispered about her love life, her money, her face and whatever else became a topic of interest. She made sure never to let on that the whispering bothered her.

"It sure looks like her," the woman in pink replied in more hushed tones. "But with that hat I can't be sure."

College T-shirt nodded with growing excitement. "Yes, yes. I think that's her."

Hot Pink nudged her. "Dora, lower your voice. She might hear you."

"She can't hear us, Trish. Wow, I wonder what she's doing here. I haven't seen her lately. She used to be everywhere—TV, magazines."

"What do you think happened?"

To Mariella's annoyance Dora lowered her tone. She leaned closer to hear. "Oh yes. Now I remember. It was a big scandal. I heard she was having an affair with Jeremiah Cooper."

"The mysterious owner of *Flash* magazine?"

"No, you're thinking of Ian. His son. Jeremiah Cooper is the photographer."

"Oh yeah, I've seen his work. He's dead now, right?"

"Yes, they weren't together long, but I'm sure he was a bad influence."

"He may have been a bad influence, but everyone knows about her temper." Suddenly Trish's voice became excited. "Isn't that Lizbeth, the famous Nigerian model?" Both women got a glimpse of a tall dark model entering a white limousine.

"Yes, let's try to get a closer look." Their voices

faded away. But they were too late, the car took off quickly and the windows were tinted. Lizbeth had arrived early to have several independent pictures taken with Mariella, and was off to yet another shoot.

Mariella sighed. She knew about the rumors and nasty headlines, which were mostly wrong or blown out of proportion. However, the media kept her in the spotlight and while she knew that everyone had misinterpreted her relationship with Jeremiah, she didn't mind the deception. Jeremiah Cooper had been her mentor and had introduced her to the right people and helped her new career at a time when she needed a change. She had met him at a reception for Desire's top models. He was an internationally known photographer, who was known for going through women—models in particular—with an unmatched ferocity. She remembered how he had approached her at the event. A tall, impeccably dressed figure in a crushed velvet blue jacket that made everyone else look dull in comparison.

"Are you as bored as I am?" he asked her.

"That depends on what's boring you."

He sent her a sly look and began to grin. Their host rushed up to them delighted. "Oh, you two have found each other. I wanted—"

Jeremiah waved her away. "There's no need to introduce us. I know who she is and she should know who I am."

"Really?" Mariella said, amused by his bold statement.

"Yes, you strike me as an educated woman with incredible taste."

"And you strike me as a charming man of incredible discernment."

He took her arm and led her away. "Let's find out more about each other."

He didn't have to persuade her. Unlike many of the male suitors who had approached her that evening, he wasn't, or didn't appear to be, shaken by her beauty. The brief meeting had blossomed into a genuine friendship, and while she did not doubt his reputation with women, their relationship was one of friendship. Thankfully, with his help it hadn't hurt as much when Desire didn't renew her contract and modeling jobs became scarce.

Some had speculated that it was because she was over thirty, others because of her difficult reputation, while others just thought her time had passed. Fortunately, she'd moved on.

By that time, modeling had lost its joy for her. She had gotten weary of living out of a suitcase and traveling the globe. At first she had enjoyed the attention, the money, the glamour of meeting interesting people and many other perks. She had been invited to dine with some of the most eligible bachelors in the world, and none of them had been shy in expressing their adulation of her, and why they wanted her as their "catch." And Mariella had played along. She was used to it.

They showered her with gifts, jewelry, designer clothes (not that she really needed them), exotic trips and vacations, and yes, she'd had some very good lovers. But that was as far as it went. Lovers were manageable, boyfriends could be a hassle. Her mother's advice, to take what she could, when she could, was a constant reminder not to be bait in an industry full of sharks.

She remembered one photo shoot that nearly ended her life. In that particular situation, she was required to have a tiger lie beside her. She had been told that it was tame, but when a flash of light spooked it, the tiger became agitated and went after her. Luckily, the handlers were able to subdue the tiger before he could do extensive damage, although she had required hospitalization and had to have stitches in her leg. The injury required plastic surgery to get the scar cosmetically fixed. Then there was the photo shoot she did in Bermuda with a well-known photographer who tried to take advantage of her. She, in turn, left him with a nasty scar.

But those days were behind her. She now had a new career and would succeed at it. She would make Jeremiah proud.

Hillary, the makeup artist, tentatively approached her holding up an eyeliner pencil as though it were a sword. "Um…I—?"

Mariella held up a hand. "Do you have a problem?"

Hillary cowered as though expecting a blow. "Yes."

"Have you come up with ten solutions on your own that haven't worked?"

"Um…no."

"Then come to me when you have."

"Okay," Hillary squeaked. She turned and walked a few feet then stopped and spun back. "But—"

"What?" Mariella snapped.

"Elena has fainted."

Mariella glanced up and saw one of the models spread out like a fallen scarecrow. "Then pick her up. She's not much use to us lying flat on her face, is she?" Hillary nodded, then dashed away.

Gen rushed up to Mariella, anxiety evident in her voice. "We could be dealing with heatstroke soon."

"No, we won't," Mariella said, as though she had the ability to prevent it.

Suddenly a loud scream cut through Gen's reply. The two women turned as another scream pierced the air.

Mariella spun around. "What the hell is that?"

Gen sighed. "It's Damien."

She turned and saw her hairstylist, a grim little man with large hands, pacing back and forth.

Mariella walked up to him. "What is wrong with you?"

He looked up at her with tears swimming in his small green eyes. "I can't do this."

"Yes, you can."

"The sun is against me. Their hair is falling flat from the sweat. Their makeup is beginning to streak, and…" His voice broke. "I can't take this anymore."

Mariella smiled her voice deceptively serene. "Yes, you can. Do you know why?"

He shook his head.

"Because I said so. You know how I feel about nervous breakdowns. "

He threw up his hands in despair. "But I can't. It's like trying to build a sundae in an oven."

"Do you remember Rome? And the fact that I saved your career?"

His eyes widened and color drained from his face. His green eyes brightened with fear.

Mariella nodded, pleased. "I see that you do. Good. Now, everything is going to be perfect, right?"

He swallowed, his Adam's apple quivering.

"Right?"

He wiped his brow then nodded.

"Great. You can go now."

He hurried away.

Gen shook her head as she watched him go. "You shouldn't be so hard on him."

"I don't have time for a man going into hysterics."

"He can't help that it's hot."

"It's not that hot," Mariella said, ignoring the trickle of sweat rolling down her back. She had to remain calm. She was the one in charge and others would follow her example. She needed to think. She motioned to Hillary who scuttled over to her.

"Yes?"

"Tell them to take off their coats and mufflers and take a break until he shows," she said, trying not to focus on the time wasted. Budget costs she hadn't anticipated. She leaned against a tree wishing she had the strength to uproot and throw it.

"You could shoot around him," Gen suggested.

"Right now I feel like shooting him. Point blank."

"Mariella…"

"I can't show 'Romantic winter fun' with just female models. It's not that kind of magazine."

"But the temperature is rising every minute."

"I know. I have to get this done. I haven't scheduled more time and Lizbeth is off to Japan tomorrow. It was the only time I could get her."

Mariella looked past Gen and saw a model stumble then fall. She rubbed her temple trying to ease a building headache. She was doing a major catalog shoot with a missing male model, a psychotic hairstylist and a makeup artist trying to keep models from collapsing. There was one bright spot. The day couldn't get any worse.

"I don't think this is a good idea." Josh Cooper sent a nervous look at his brother who casually drove his Jeep down the highway. "We don't have to meet her. We could call her over the phone."

Ian rested his arm on the door frame, a grin touching his lips. "You're afraid of her."

"Terrified."

He clicked his tongue in sympathy. "That's your problem. Fear gives her the upper hand."

"My fear keeps me safe."

"You've dealt with models before."

Josh turned to look at his brother. Ian looked calm and relaxed—two things he was not. But Josh couldn't read him with Ian's mirrored sunglasses shielding his eyes. No surprise, Ian never revealed more of himself than he wanted to. However, Josh knew Ian was not happy with their father's will. He wasn't too happy with it either since it meant dealing with Mariella. Josh groaned, wishing he could make Ian understand the severity of the situation. "Yes, I've worked with models. Even slept with a few, but I've never met one like her. I've worked with her exactly twice and nearly had my balls swinging around my neck."

"She's no different than the typical overprivileged, half-starved divas that fill the industry."

"Don't underestimate her, Ian. You have to help me out here. Gen doesn't—" He stopped, looking guilty.

Ian hid a grin. "So you're still in love with a woman who barely knows you exist?"

"She does know I exist," Josh grumbled, though he felt his neck grow hot.

"Which is why you've had such a beautiful long-distance relationship where you idolize her and she walks past you."

"She's shy and close to Mariella. I haven't gotten a chance to make my move."

"Why not?"

"We're not sure Mariella would approve."

"Is she her mother?"

"Mariella helped Gen out of a tough situation and she feels beholden."

"How did she help her?"

Josh shrugged, already feeling defeated. "She won't say, but if you could keep Mariella busy, I could make my move."

"Make your move now. What could Mariella do to you?"

Josh looked horrified. "Do you want me to have nightmares?"

Ian shook his head and sighed.

Josh made an attempt to shake off the terrible image he had of what damage Mariella could do to him then said, "Just make me look good. I really want to convince her that things will be fine."

"They will be fine," Ian said with quiet certainty.

"You haven't met Mariella yet. I tell you she is different."

"And you haven't told me *how* different."

"Well," he said with careful consideration. "She's domineering, smart, vicious."

Ian looked bored. "And that makes her different how?"

Josh's shoulders slumped. "You'd have to meet her."

Ian smiled. "I plan to." At that moment, Ian saw the sign to the park and the lush shrubbery lining the entrance. "If she's going to work for me, she'll have to know her place."

"You don't even know if she'll say yes."

Ian's smile grew, his white teeth gleaming. "Yes, I do."

Josh shook his head, worried by his brother's confidence. "But Ian—"

Ian parked the car, jumped out and shut the door. "She won't be any different than the other women Dad has had in his life."

"So you think the rumors are true?"

"You heard the will."

"Yes," he said, his mouth set in a grim line.

"A man doesn't make a special request like that for just any woman."

"I still can't believe it." Josh hesitated. "Dad wasn't really his old self toward the end. You don't know since—" He stopped midsentence, but that didn't halt the tension that suddenly settled between them. Ian's absence and their father's will were sore subjects Ian didn't like to discuss. Josh knew that his brother could be a real SOB when he wanted to. Josh gripped his fists, ready for whatever was to come. Meanwhile, Ian scanned the park looking relaxed and did not reply. When he finally did, his voice was laced with venom.

"Don't ever bring up that subject again."

Josh swallowed. "Right."

Ian motioned to something in the distance. "I think I see her." He spotted a striking woman in white with a big pinwheel hat.

Josh's heart began to race. "Yes, that's her."

"I guess I'd better go over and..." Ian's words faded away when she turned to look at them. Even from a distance her beauty was mesmerizing. "Maybe I won't have to."

"No." Josh took a step back. "It looks like she's coming this way."

Chapter 2

Yes, come to me. Ian watched Mariella, a rush of anticipation gripping him as she came closer. Something seized and paralyzed him and it wasn't fear, but he refused to give it a name. She moved like a model, not the exaggerated gait of the catwalk, but in a manner that commanded attention. She definitely had his.

Josh took another step back. "She looks furious."

"Yes, and if you take another step back you won't have to worry about her."

Josh halted.

Ian continued to watch her. He'd once witnessed a wildlife special where a lioness devoured a wildebeest. Mariella looked as though she could do worse. She stopped a foot away from him. From a distance she was breathtaking. Up close her exquisite beauty was undeniable. From the curve of her chin to the shape of her figure she was a vision to behold. *But the words out of her mouth were anything but.* "You're late," she said, her clear brown eyes piercing the dark shield of his sunglasses.

Ian rested his hands on his hips. "Ms. Duvall—"

"I don't have time for your excuses," she interrupted. "When I say a shoot is at a certain time, I expect you to be there. You're not even what I expected." She walked around him as though she were a judge at an animal show. "My God, you're enormous. You'll throw the balance off completely. I may have to put the girls on rocks or something. Remove those sunglasses so that I can get a better look at you."

"Ms. Duvall—"

"I said remove them." She reached up to do it herself; Ian gripped her wrist before she could.

"That wouldn't be a good idea," he said quietly.

She pulled her wrist free. "Why not?"

"Because I don't like people to touch me."

"You'll get over it." She lifted his chin. "You have a wonderful profile."

Ian heard his brother snicker and frowned. Josh covered his mouth and coughed.

His cough caught Mariella's attention. "I didn't expect you to be here."

"No," Josh said. He awkwardly gestured to Ian. "Well, he's—"

"Your friend no doubt. Perhaps on the drive back you can teach him how to tell time." She turned to Ian again. "You'll do. Now go over there." She pointed to the wardrobe area. There were several freestanding clothes racks with an assortment of designer clothing. "Get into the wool set immediately."

Josh opened his mouth to protest. "But he's not—"

She waved a dismissive hand, making it clear that she'd lost interest in them. "That's it for now." She turned and stalked off.

Ian stood for a moment with his hands on his hips.

Josh shook his head and watched her go. "I told you she'd be difficult." He turned to Ian. "I don't—" he began, then noticed the slight grin on his brother's face. "You think this is funny?" he asked amazed.

"I think this is hilarious." He rubbed the smile from his face. "Excuse me." Ian jogged up to Mariella and darted in front of her with such speed that she crashed into him. She stumbled back, her hat falling to the ground. Ian bent down, quickly retrieved it then held it out to her as a peace offering.

Mariella angrily snatched her hat out of his hand. "What is wrong with you? Why aren't you in wardrobe? First you arrive twenty minutes late, and now it appears that you can't follow simple directions."

"I need to talk to you."

Mariella placed her hands on her hips, her eyes blazing with a heat that could rival the day. "I don't know what your problem is, who you are, or why you were hired for this shoot. Now, before I lose my temper altogether, if you plan on being paid for this assignment, I suggest you get into your outfit as quickly as you can." She turned ready to walk away. Ian again positioned himself in front of her.

She narrowed her eyes and said in a low voice, "Move."

He folded his arms.

She moved to the other side, he blocked her again. She scowled; he smiled.

His hands fell to his waist. "I'll let you pass when I feel that I've gotten my point across."

"You'll move now or—"

He lifted a challenging brow. "Or what?"

"I'll make your life a living hell," she said in an acid tone.

He hooked his thumbs in his jeans pockets and took a step forward. "Is that a promise?"

She took a step toward him. "It's a guarantee."

He closed the distance between them, their noses nearly touching. "I like guarantees, but know this: Whatever you can dish out, I can do worse."

Mariella tried to stare past the mirrored shield of his dark glasses. "I bet you're not so tough without sunglasses."

"No, I'm meaner."

Josh cleared his throat, hoping to get their attention. He coughed. When that didn't work, he caught Gen's eye and gestured to the pair. Recognizing the situation, Gen quickly rushed over to help.

"Mariella, what's going on?"

She turned to Gen and jerked a thumb at Ian. "This person has an attitude." She shot a rude glance at him. "You won't last long in this industry."

Gen nervously gripped her clipboard. "Mariella, don't you know who he is?"

"I don't care who he is. Gen, take over. I need him in the full wool suit, with the fur-lined hooded jacket. Let's see how long he can remain cool. And have him report to me in the gazebo in five minutes. Lucky for him, he doesn't appear to need much makeup. We'll shoot him as is, I can always touch up the photo later. He's wasted enough of my—our time." Mariella adjusted her hat. "Have the models get back into their outfits, and have

Damien get them ready. He has exactly four
minutes." Without looking back, Mariella walked
off. Ian remained standing, in silence. Gen ran
after her.

"Mariella, you've made a big mistake."

"Now what? The only big mistake I see is that
I should have selected the male model myself.
Where did you find this jerk? I thought you had
better taste, Gen. But one thing I can promise you,
once this shoot is over, I'm going to make sure that
he's finished in this industry."

"But that's Ian Cooper," Gen said.

She furrowed her brows, finding the name
vaguely familiar. "Ian Cooper? I suppose that is
supposed to mean something to me?"

"He's my brother," Josh said, from behind.

"Jeremiah Cooper's other son," Gen added.

"Ian?" Mariella blinked. "Ian Cooper, the
new owner of *Flash* magazine?" Mariella looked
over her shoulder at the dark, quiet figure. She
softly swore then approached him. "You're Ian
Cooper?"

He nodded.

She coolly measured him, her eyes falling to his
feet then rising to his face. "Oh, yes. I see," she said
in a tone that hinted that she wished she hadn't.
"That one. Your father told me a little about you."

Ian cocked his head to the side. "Unfortunately,
I didn't have the same pleasure."

"Well, it would be hard to hear things when you're not around," she said.

Josh saw his brother's face change and quickly stepped forward. "Perhaps we've come at a bad time."

Ian didn't move and neither did Mariella.

Gen looked at Josh helplessly, then saw a tall figure in the distance. "I think the model's here," she announced as though her savior had appeared on the horizon.

Mariella turned and saw a handsome young man in worn jeans with a khaki jacket thrown carelessly over his shoulder. "Gen, take care of him. He doesn't really look the part, but he'll have to do. I want him ready in three minutes. But first I'll have a few words." Mariella looked at Ian one last time to say something then decided against it and left. She approached the young model, her hands waving frantically in the air, her displeasure evident.

Josh gave a low whistle. "Man, I'd hate to be him," he said a few minutes later as he watched the male model leap into position, posing awkwardly between the three women. Mariella began the shoot with a frenzy, totally oblivious to the audience she had attracted. She was at her best when she was taking pictures and giving orders. Whenever she was on a job, her intensity heightened and so did the fear of those around her. No shoot was ever good enough, and she would take picture after picture, until she felt she had captured what she wanted. And she was especially hard on the male model that had arrived late.

"Have you ever modeled before?" she asked him, not expecting an answer. She positioned him atop the small bridge, with his arm around one model, and the rest of his body angled in a way that looked rather impossible.

He tried not to grimace. "I don't think I can hold this position for very long," he responded, but was not given an answer. Instead, Mariella continued directing the females, and ignoring him completely.

"You can actually see him shrinking," Josh said with sympathy. "If she doesn't stop soon, she'll have nothing to photograph."

"At least he's here," Gen said.

When Ian didn't reply, Josh turned to him. His brother hadn't moved. Josh shifted awkwardly. "Perhaps we'd better go. We can talk to her another time."

"I'm not going anywhere." He folded his arms. "What is this photo shoot for again?"

"The upcoming Bretton winter catalog," Gen said.

"I see."

"I don't," Josh said. "Dad said she was good. But I don't see why he wants us to give a prime exclusive contract to a woman who does staged catalog photography and layouts for obscure magazines and celebrity portraits."

"Mariella is an excellent photographer," Gen said defensively. "She has had top celebrities ask for her specifically to do their portraits. Her work is quickly making its rounds in different venues. Your father knew she would be a top photographer. He saw her talent right away."

"I'm sorry," Josh said surprised by her vehemence.

Gen lowered her head, embarrassed. "I didn't mean to jump on you like that. It's just that I don't like when people are so quick to judge her. She really is a good person and is extremely talented. We're not just a bunch of dumb ex-models no matter what other people think."

"I don't think many people think that anymore," he said gently. "At least I don't. I didn't mean to deny that she had talent. But I do know one thing."

"What?"

Josh flashed a slow smile. "I can see that she has a good friend."

"Gen, are you interested in working?" Mariella barked, grasping the camera slung over her shoulder. "You can visit with your friend on your own time."

Gen touched her earring with nervous fingers. "Yes, well…I'd better get back to work."

"Yeah," Josh said wistfully. He watched her go then turned to Ian. "Do you see my problem? She's devoted to Mariella."

"Hmm," Ian said then walked over to a magnolia tree and sat under it. He hadn't taken his gaze off of Mariella.

Josh sat beside him. "But if you can keep Mariella busy with that new photo assignment, I'll get my chance."

"Hmm," Ian said again. He hadn't removed his gaze from Mariella. She moved well. She would. Like all models she was a chameleon and could fit into any situation. Today she was every bit the photographer. He could see that. But she captured everything he abhorred: Models, staged settings and staid objects like trees and streams.

He liked action. He couldn't help it. He was still a photojournalist at heart. If he'd had his camera he wouldn't be taking pictures of the trees or the models. He'd take a picture of the little man, sweating furiously, wiping his forehead with one hand and blowing his nose into a handkerchief with the other. Or the bleach-blond assistant fanning one of the models dressed in a bulky hand-knit sweater, fitted wool leggings, suede mittens and fur hat; another trying to stave off a bee circling overhead. But mostly he'd photograph the woman at the center of all the action. He had to admit that she was commanding in her role. Mariella left no scene untouched, bending in whatever position was needed to capture a certain angle, barking out orders and drinking a sports drink between commands.

He had to admire her. For all her beauty and grace, she had no problem lying down on the grass, holding a difficult position from a branch of a tree or wading in the small stream. His fingers itched for the first time, in a long time, to hold a camera. He'd given up photography to run the company. When his father had fallen ill and asked him to take over, he knew his duty would be to step in, while his father recuperated.

Jeremiah had fought against the pancreatic cancer. But it wasn't the cancer that killed him. Ian tapped his knee; he didn't want to think about it. The wound was still tender, more than he'd allow himself to admit Now he only did photography as a hobby. He hadn't wanted to photograph someone like this since… He shook his head and softly swore.

"What's wrong?" Josh asked.

"Nothing," he lied, adjusting his sunglasses. A sinking feeling slithered through him. He had a bad feeling that he and his father had developed the same taste in women.

Chapter 3

When the shoot was finally over, Mariella wanted to collapse with relief. This feeling fled quickly, however, when she noticed the two figures in the distance. She'd expected them to have left. No, that was wrong, she'd hoped *he* had left. Josh she could handle, Ian was another issue entirely. She could feel him staring at her. She was used to men staring, but never with such intensity. Never with such brazen determination to make his presence known. She felt like a prisoner in spite of the distance that separated them.

Perhaps she was wrong. Perhaps he wasn't looking at her at all. She couldn't tell since he still had his sunglasses on. She glanced at them again. No, she was certain he was watching her. She suddenly felt grateful for the sunglasses—they created a nice barrier.

She looked at Josh who was busy trying to swat away a cloud of gnats. Mariella had never seen brothers so dissimilar, but then that's what people thought when they saw her and her younger sister Isabella. Josh was of a slighter build. Although tall, his build was far from intimidating. He had awkward, yet warm features: an angular nose, nice mouth, ordinary eyes and ears that were a little too large. No one would call him handsome or even attractive, but he didn't have to be because he was smart, rich and had a famous father.

Ian, on the other hand, was gorgeous. She reluctantly used the term to describe him, but it was accurate. He reminded her of a puma—if a puma were to become a man in jeans and a black T-shirt that fit like a second skin and emphasized a well-sculpted chest. Interestingly, he looked like a man who wore his clothes for comfort rather than vanity. Mariella decided that her first assessment of him was accurate. Although he was not the model for the shoot, he was too large, too arrogant and just too much of everything to be a good model or a good man for that matter. Jeremiah had been a devil. Ian was probably ten times worse.

For a moment, Mariella wondered what his

eyes looked like, but she sensed that being curious about him was dangerous. She brushed the thought aside. His presence was already a nuisance.

Mariella began to gather her things together, ready to leave. The rest of the crew had left thirty minutes earlier; she was the only one there. To her dismay she saw the puma slowly rise and come toward her. He covered the distance quickly and quietly, sending goose bumps up her arms despite the warm day.

"Not bad," Ian said.

She continued to pack her equipment.

"Some of your angles will be off, you're not an expert on how to use lighting yet, but no one will look too closely. All that matters are the clothes."

She zipped up her camera bag. "Everything was perfect."

"You don't believe that and neither do I. It's okay, you were nervous, but hid it well."

"I wasn't nervous."

"Do you miss it?"

She blinked. "Miss what?"

"Modeling."

"No. I'm a photographer now."

"Not out of choice."

"Of course it was a choice. I chose it."

He shook his head. "Let's stop playing games. We both know why your career ended."

"It ended because I decided to end it."

"That's not what I heard."

"Then I suggest you get your hearing checked."

"There's nothing wrong with my ears, but there may be something wrong with your memory."

"I don't think so."

He was quiet a moment. "No, you wouldn't." He turned his head to stare at something, but made no movement to leave.

Mariella opened her mouth then closed it. She sighed and folded her arms impatiently. "What do you want?"

He turned to her and smiled. "Thank you for asking. Your consideration will be a great asset when we're working together."

"I never said I'd work with you."

He wagged a finger and shook his head. "*For* me, not with me."

"It doesn't matter," she said nonchalantly.

"It will." He held out his card. "I want you to come to my office."

"I don't think—"

"You're not a stupid woman, Ms. Duvall. Don't act like one for my enjoyment. I have a proposition that could catapult your career."

"I don't model anymore."

"I'm interested in your photography."

"I see," she said, trying to keep a handle on her

growing excitement. "Do you want to start where your father left off?"

Ian became very still. "Is that an offer?"

Mariella wondered about his strange response then remembered how her words could be misinterpreted. "Regarding photography? Yes."

"Meet me in my office, tomorrow at eleven and I'll explain my proposition. And see if we can come to an understanding." He turned and left.

Mariella stared at his card, resisting an urge to jump with triumph. She couldn't believe it. What an opportunity. Perhaps *Flash* magazine wanted to use some of her celebrity portraits. Maybe Jeremiah spoke to Ian before he died. Slowly her mounting joy began to fade. But it was obvious that, just like the others, Ian thought that her relationship with Jeremiah was different than it was. Although that image had served its purpose in the past, Mariella didn't want to use it now. She gathered up her belongings, and threw them in a large mesh bag lying next to her, and dashed after him. She caught Ian as he was about to get into his car.

"There's something you should know."

He stopped halfway. "Yes?"

She glanced at Josh then Ian. "I know what the papers said, but they weren't always right. Your father and I were friends. He helped me with my photography. There was never anything more between us. So if this is some kind of bribe in order to keep me quiet about something that wasn't true, there's no need." She waited, ready to hand him back the card. While Jeremiah had been alive, she had gotten many offers, only to find out that they usually wanted more than her photography talent. Many assumed she was a certain type of woman based on her relationship with Jeremiah. It had angered her on several occasions because some of the "contacts" Jeremiah considered to be his trusted friends and colleagues, were the worst, and she had never had the nerve to tell him.

"I see."

Mariella hesitated, not sure what those two words meant. "Does that change anything?"

The corner of his mouth kicked up. "That changes everything." He got into his car. "See you at eleven," he said then sped away.

Mariella entered her place exhausted and ready to collapse on the couch, but the savory aromas coming from the kitchen renewed her spirit. "Dinner's ready," Gen called out. "Do you want to take a shower first? Or are you ready now?" Before she could finish her sentence, Mariella had found her way to the kitchen and was already trying to sneak one of Gen's spicy stuffed cabbages. Mariella's favorite.

"Mariella," Gen playfully scolded.

"Just one bite."

"Okay," she said.

Gen was Mariella's perfect roommate. Being a former model helped. She knew the pressures of the industry, the competition, the drive, and her experience of living in a model's apartment at sixteen helped her become self-sufficient and know how to handle living with others and hustle when necessary. And as Mariella's assistant she was ready for action at any time.

Mariella knew that Gen played a much greater role than her title credited her with, but that didn't bother her, especially since Mariella was a very generous boss when it came to her salary. They lived in a trendy three-bedroom, two-level condominium, with an exquisite view of the Hudson River. While they were very different in temperament, they both shared a love of art.

Mariella's interest in art had been greatly expanded when she had worked at an art gallery in upstate N.Y., and she spent most of her discretionary funds buying unique and exclusive pieces. Shopping for art was her second love, next to buying cosmetics. The hallway entrance, with its twelve-foot skylighted ceiling was a showcase of black-and-white photographs, which included several signed copies by Jeremiah.

Throughout the shared space, the walls were painted a soft blue, with eggshell white trim, and an eclectic array of furniture. In the living room, with its vaulted ceiling and high windows, was a long teak couch, with overstuffed maroon cushions, an assortment of oil paintings, one-of-a-kind blown glass lamps, and two high-back artist chairs.

Mariella went directly to her room, still high from the potential offer. Her room was her oasis, with calming colors, pared-down décor, and richly textured accessories. With a large picture window facing the Hudson, her walls were covered with cream brocade-textured wallpaper. On one large wall, there were framed pictures of some of her most memorable cover shots, and of course the ones that made her look the best, even though none ever made her look bad. Dispersed in between were mirrors, of varying sizes and shapes, adding an element of fantasy.

Off to the side, was a three-way mirror and a Japanese Shoshi screen. On her large oak chest and jewelry armoire, were numerous photos of her sisters, their families and her parents, in an assortment of gold frames. Her matching bedroom set included a large poster bed with voluminous white curtains, tastefully adorned with cashmere throws and linen pillows, providing soft touches. And of course, there was excellent lighting, provided by ornate track lighting that could be adjusted to either daylight or evening lighting, at the touch of a button.

Above the bed was a prized possession Jeremiah had given her: a three-photo series of children playing. Mariella walked into her bathroom—a sleek, upscale alcove with every comfort money could buy. Her makeup table looked like the backstage at a theater. There were numerous books on makeup and characterization, and pictures, with instructions on how to get a wide array of looks.

Although she always had makeup and hair professionals at each shoot, Mariella was known as being very gifted in doing her own. As a child growing up, she had practiced for hours, changing her look and appearance, using her mother's makeup. Once she went so far as cutting her hair into a really short do. Needless to say, her new hairstyle did not go over well with her mother, and from then on she practiced on her dolls instead. When it came to having the look, Mariella always had everything on hand.

That night after a quick shower, and hurried dinner, Mariella completed the paperwork for the Bretton shoot, then she went on her laptop determined to find out everything she could about Ian Cooper. She told herself she was just curious to find out about the man she might be working with. She didn't want to admit that he intrigued her. From the dark glasses that shielded his eyes to the dark shirt that emphasized his build, he was a man of mystery.

She remembered that Jeremiah rarely talked about Ian and she'd never seen a picture of him anywhere. Even after he'd taken over the magazine he hadn't allowed his picture to be shown in the paper. When Jeremiah did speak about his son, it was in general terms and he only referred to Ian's temper and recklessness—the words were usually spoken with both pride and pain. She knew about Josh from the start. Josh was always there. But who was Ian? And why did he want to work with her? Was Jeremiah behind it?

Mariella entered her query online, determined to find out more. What she uncovered left her speechless. Ian had been an award-winning photojournalist for nearly ten years. His photographs had been featured on the covers of *Fortune* and *National Geographic*. He'd covered the Olympics, several wars, and both natural and man-made disasters. The online collection of his work astounded her. It was dark, ruthless, clear and dangerous. No light, no brilliancy of color. Stark, yet moving as though he was unaware of the compassion he'd brought to the composition.

One moving photograph showed homes decimated by a hurricane looking like toothpicks scattered in a puddle, contrasted with kids playing soccer in a FEMA trailer park nearby. Another picture showed the setting sun spreading its warmth on the devastation of a structure that had once been a home. In the middle stood the faint image of a couple embracing among the debris of their former life; yet another picture showed a silhouette of bare trees, their leaves ripped from the branches, standing tall, with the string of a deflated yellow balloon dangling from the tip of a branch, lonely and dejected. That picture shook her with an unexpected wave of sorrow although she didn't know why.

This couldn't be him. This had to be a mistake. This couldn't be the arrogant, condescending jerk she'd met today. A man like him couldn't portray such humanity, show reality with such tender cruelty and gentle pain. She could see that he was as talented, if not more, than his father. Yet, his work was so different than Jeremiah's. Jeremiah approached photography with a light fanciful air. Almost as a game, which was why she had enjoyed working with him. He'd taught her to feel the image through the lens. To not be afraid to arrange a scene, or to create one, no matter how contrived it looked. The final outcome was what counted.

The emotion the photographer wanted to capture and impart to the viewer was paramount. Jeremiah had been markedly different than her father who had given her a camera at eight and said "Take a picture of anything so that I can see what you see," his island accent caressing each word. He'd found beauty in the strangest, ordinary places—a broken leaf, footsteps in the snow, not feeling the need to alter them. Unlike her mother, he didn't emphasize her beauty. Instead, he taught her, along with her three other sisters, to enjoy as much as they could, and that beauty was all around them.

She hadn't been a very good student of his philosophy. On her mother's insistence, she had focused more on refining her social skills, and had to admit she liked all the attention, but there were times when she wasn't attending some recital, or taking tap and voice lessons, that she would be outside taking pictures.

Of course, her mother never approved and always reminded her that she should be in front of the camera, not behind it. Her father had understood her. He was probably the only one who did, beside her sister Isabella. He knew and nourished her love of taking pictures and would always tell her that if she ever wanted to do something different, that she would make a good photographer. She never dreamed that one day it would come true.

Oddly, Ian's approach to photography wasn't like her father's or Jeremiah's. Ian approached it like a storyteller for future generations to uncover and for present ones to reflect on. Looking at his pictures made her want to be better, not just good, but great.

Mariella stayed online for the rest of the evening, reading Ian's articles on photography. His prose was as deep, intelligent and mesmerizing as his photographs.

"What are you doing?" Gen asked, clutching a cup of warm Ovaltine. She pulled up a chair next to Mariella who sat hunched over her laptop at the dining room table. Lights from the town shone brightly into the apartment casting soft shadows on the walls. "You've been on that thing since finishing dinner."

"I'm reading about Ian Cooper. He used to be a photojournalist."

"I know."

Mariella didn't ask her how she knew, that wasn't the question that plagued her. "Why did he give up all this to run a magazine?"

"He had to," Gen said. "Josh told me he had to step in when his father became ill, because the magazine wasn't doing well and they knew Ian could turn things around."

Jeremiah hadn't told her that. But he never discussed business with her. "I wonder what he could want with me."

"Ian wants to meet with you?"

"Yes. He gave me his card and said to come to his office tomorrow at eleven."

"You'll have to ask him then."

"Don't worry. I intend to."

"I'm sure Josh—" She stopped.

Mariella couldn't help a smile. "Josh seems to have a lot to say."

"We spoke a little at the park."

"I see."

"It's nothing serious," Gen said quickly.

"Funny you should say that because I keep having this strange feeling that you're in love with him."

Gen's face reddened. "Why would you say that?"

"I won't say it if you tell me I'm wrong."

Gen sipped her drink then set the cup down. "I know he's not what you'd call handsome but *I* like his looks, and that's all that matters; plus he's smart and sweet and…" She picked up the cup.

"And?" Mariella pressed.

She stared down at the cup. "Yes, I do love him."

Mariella rested her chin in her hand and shook her head. "Don't move too fast."

Gen frowned. "Why?"

"It's been my experience that people rarely make rational decisions when in the 'I'm in love' state. Trust me, I've seen my sisters do bizarre things because of it."

"Sounds romantic to me," Gen said softly.

Mariella sat back and pointed at her. "Listen, because of love, some of what they did looked ridiculous at the time. Fortunately, everything worked out. All I can say is I hope to leave this planet without falling prey to it."

"You've never been in love?"

"No, nor do I plan to be. That doesn't mean I'm not capable of loving. I love my sisters and nephews and niece very much." She smiled. "And you, of course."

Gen didn't smile back. She looked at Mariella as though she'd happened upon a strange creature. "So you never want to get married?"

"What made you think that?"

"Well, you said—"

"I said I never wanted to fall in love. I didn't say I'd never marry. Marriage can be very advantageous if it is to the right person."

"If you love him, it's the right person."

"Not necessarily. A man should always love a woman more. Otherwise the woman is at a disadvantage."

"How can that be?"

"Love makes you weak, vulnerable. Women only have few powers to claim, and giving away our hearts leads to our greatest oppression."

"I don't believe that."

"You don't have to but it's true. Why is it that the best love stories usually deal with someone dying? I'll tell you: Because men believe in sacrifice and suffering, especially when it comes to a woman's lot in life. Suicide, ruination, depression,

death, illness. All the classics have women who
don't, or cannot survive, without the 'love' in their
lives, or lovers separated by fate who will do
anything to be together, including killing themselves."

"But love stories—"

Mariella held up a hand silencing her. "Personally, I find them as realistic as a unicorn, but that's
just me. We can dream of men who will risk all
for us as much as we risk for them *but* those
stories only exist in books. I am a realist and plan
to keep myself intact by living in a rational
manner. Either marry a man who adores you—
one you can reasonably tolerate—or don't get
married at all."

Gen stared at her friend, amazed. "Mariella,
how can you be so cynical? I thought you said
your sisters are happily married."

"They are, but they are the type of women who
make good wives. I don't. I'm aware of my faults.
I can be impatient and demanding and I'm certainly not the nurturing motherly type that men
crave. The best husband for me would be a man
who is very rich and travels a lot."

"I believe that men and women can love each
other equally."

Mariella shrugged. "Well, you can choose to
believe that if you want to. Do you think Josh
loves you?"

"I don't know," Gen stammered. "I think he likes me."

"Likes you? Don't be modest. I've seen him tripping over his feet, and he's always tongue-tied when he's around you. I suppose he'll suit you. No, he's not very handsome, but at least he's rich."

"Mariella, don't talk like that," Gen scolded.

"I'm just being honest. You know as well as I do that men are visual creatures. Right? Well, look at you. You're beautiful, and you've been an international model. You can get any man you want, you have the looks, so use them. It doesn't matter for what."

Gen shifted awkwardly in her seat. "But it makes you sound shallow."

"Who's to say I'm not?"

"I know you're not," she said firmly. "If you were, I wouldn't be your roommate. Besides, if you were truly shallow you wouldn't have been staring at those photos all evening."

Mariella glanced at her watch. "Has it been that long? What time is it?"

"12:30 a.m. If you want to be ready for your appointment with him tomorrow, you will need to look rested."

"Yes." Mariella turned off the screen and closed the laptop. "Well, his work is impressive, I'll give him that." She walked over to the stove, and poured herself a cup of tea. "But we're not talking about me," she said, determined to continue their prior topic.

Gen sighed, looking a lot older than her twenty-four years. "How I feel about Josh doesn't matter."

"You're concerned about how he feels about you?"

"No." Gen lowered her head. "You know that I can't be with any man."

"Your past—"

Gen met her eyes. "Is part of who I am. I can't lie about it, but I don't want to reveal it either."

"He shouldn't mind. This is a new day."

"It's not that new. There are still certain taboos. I don't think Josh would be able to handle it. Besides, look at the kind of family he comes from. Yes, I know what you're probably going to say. I may have the looks, but unlike you, Mariella, I don't have your kind of confidence. Men love the way I look, and for many, they think I'm a certain way, when I'm not. And…" She went to the sink and dumped the contents of her cup. "You know, I really don't want to talk about it anymore. Trust me, I know it won't work."

"How would you know, if you don't give him the chance?"

"I don't want to know." Gen abruptly turned. "Good night, see you in the morning."

Mariella sat back at the table then turned the

laptop on again, this time wondering which of her photos would impress Mr. Ian Cooper. Mariella spent most of the night, into the early morning going through her portfolio and selecting her best photographs. She intended to get the job, and wasn't going to take any chances.

Chapter 4

Ian walked into the offices of *Flash* magazine the next morning pleased to see everyone working diligently. Just the way he liked it. Little did he know that several minutes before he entered, Merta Robinson had glanced out her office window and seen him walking toward the entrance of the building. "Oh no," she cried. "He's early."

"Why?" someone asked.

"It doesn't matter why. Places, everyone."

In a moment, people removed their feet from their desks, hid breakfast bars and donuts, and stacks of magazines, grabbed phones and exited certain Internet sites. By the time Ian entered the office with his black Labrador Sylvester at his side, the office looked like business as usual.

His assistant, Nelson Mullings, a recent college graduate and eager to please, rushed up to him. "You're early."

Ian stared at him, but didn't reply.

Nelson cleared his throat. "It was just an observation."

Ian shook his head. "No, it wasn't. You want to know why I'm coming into the office at this time. The reason is I have an appointment at eleven and I want to be ready for her."

"Oh, well, the thing is…there's a situation."

"What situation?"

"Your mother is here."

Ian paused. "In town?"

"In this building."

"Where specifically in this building?"

"In your office."

"Why?"

"Why?" Nelson echoed.

"Yes," Ian said with exaggerated patience. "Why is she in my office?"

Nelson finally understood his error. "She wanted—"

"You know I don't like people in my office when I'm not there."

"I thought I could…uh…convince her to leave before you arrived, but she insisted."

"Next time think about this. Who would you rather upset? Me or her?"

Nelson tugged on his tie, nearly strangling himself. He coughed then said, "It won't happen again."

Ian walked toward his office. "I didn't think so."

"It gets worse."

Ian stopped. "How bad?"

"She said she has luggage in the car."

"Okay." He continued walking.

"There's more."

Ian slowly spun around. "Yes?"

"She brought Candy."

He swore softly but with force. Before he could consider the perfect exit strategy, his mother stuck her head outside. "I thought I heard your voice. What's keeping you so long?" She turned her cheek to him. "Come here and kiss me hello."

"I've never kissed you hello. Stop imagining things."

"Can't you be civil for five minutes?"

"I'm assuming that's a rhetorical question." Ian turned to Nelson. "Make sure we're not disturbed." He snapped his fingers and pointed to his desk. Sylvester walked in and lay down beside it. Although he was a Lab, Sylvester was accustomed to the sedentary life in the office, which he tolerated in anticipation of the invigorating walks he took with Ian before and after his workday. Ian

followed his mother into the office and shut the
door. She sat down on the couch and held up her
cheek. He walked past.

In the absence of his greeting, she tapped her
cheek.

"Stop that," Ian said. "No one is looking so we
don't have to perform for them."

She frowned. "Other sons kiss their mothers on
the cheek."

"Yes," Ian said, sitting behind his desk and
staring at her. But other sons didn't have a mother
like Shirley Cooper. She was lavishly beautiful, a
banquet of desirable attributes: thick dark hair
with only a hint of gray despite her years, expres-
sive brown eyes that made her face look twenty
years younger, a trim figure with enough curves
to save her from being called skinny.

However, her looks hadn't kept his father from
openly playing the field, and she wasn't surprised.
His mother was a former fashion model. She had
been discovered working at her father's pharmacy
by a scout for Williamson's Modeling Agency,
and had a very successful modeling career. Before
she married his father, she knew the sacrifice she
would have to make. He had been up-front with
her, and she had weighed what was best for her.
She wanted to be taken care of and had gotten
used to the wealth and privilege that being a model
had provided. She knew that in time, she would

be too old for the industry, and wanted to ensure she would be able to continue the lifestyle she had become accustomed to. Her only regret was being passed over for a chance of being a Bond Girl.

Sitting in his office, Ian saw for a moment the beauty she must have been forty years ago. Today she wore a finely tailored pink crepe suit. But no outfit was complete without matching high-heeled Italian shoes and her Chihuahua, Candy, who sat on her lap wearing the identical suit.

Ian scowled at the dog that was dancing on its little paws eager to greet him. "Did you have to bring that?"

"Candy is very sweet and she loves you." She held up the excited dog. "Come on. Let her give you a kiss."

"The day I let her kiss me, one of us will be dead."

Shirley pulled Candy close to her chest, shielding her. "Don't be disgusting."

"So. Where are you going?"

She placed Candy on her lap and began to stroke her. "What do you mean?"

"Nelson said you brought luggage."

She lowered her gaze and adjusted Candy's jacket. "I wanted to stay with you for a few days."

"Stay with Josh."

"I don't want to stay with Josh."

"Why?"

She looked up startled. "Do I need a reason?"

"Yes."

"Your house is bigger."

"Mother," he said, losing patience. "What are you doing here?"

"Otis is getting ideas."

Ian sighed. Poor Otis Fassel. He was an international trader who had been wooing his mother for the past eight years. "What kind of ideas?"

"About marriage."

He shrugged. "So?"

"I thought we could use a little time apart."

"Why don't you just add to the man's misery and marry him?"

Shirley set Candy on the couch then crossed her legs. "I'll get married again when you do."

He began to grin. "Is that a promise?"

"Why?"

"Because that might be sooner than you think."

Her brows rose in surprise. "You're thinking of getting married again?"

He nodded.

"To whom?"

A knock on the door interrupted his reply.

"What?" Ian asked.

Nelson timidly peeked his head in. "Umm, you have a visitor."

Ian glanced at his watch. "She's early."

Nelson looked relieved. "So you are expecting her?"

"Yes, at eleven not ten."

"But since she's here now…" He let his words trail off hoping Ian would fill them in.

He leaned back and clasped his hands together. "Yes?"

"What should I do with her?"

"Nothing. She can wait."

Nelson glanced at the visitor, biting his lip then turned back to Ian. "She doesn't seem the patient type."

"She'll learn."

"But—"

"Close the door."

Nelson hesitated.

"Now."

Nelson reluctantly shut the door.

Ian leaned forward. "Where were we?"

Shirley looked at her son. "You were toying with me."

"Was I?"

"How can you talk about marriage? I haven't heard you were seeing anyone."

"The idea came to me recently."

She studied him suspiciously. "What are you up to?"

"Nothing. I'm just suggesting that you make peace with Otis. You won't have my place to run away to too much longer. I doubt my wife would like it." He paused. "Actually, I can be certain she wouldn't."

"Who is she?" Shirley said, unable to temper her curiosity. "What does she do? Where did you meet her? Is she—"

A timid knock interrupted her.

Ian sighed then said loudly, "What is it, Nelson?"

Nelson came in wringing his hands together. "Here's the thing. When it comes to patience, she's not a fast learner."

"Really?" Ian said without surprise.

"She's making things awkward."

"How awkward?"

"Merta is in tears."

Ian looked thoughtful then slowly stood. "Excuse me," he said to Shirley and followed Nelson out the door.

Almost immediately he saw Mariella gesturing to a short balding man, indicating that he needed to straighten a framed painting.

"Where's Merta?" Ian asked.

"In the kitchen," Nelson said.

Seconds later Ian stood in the kitchen where he saw Merta sitting in the corner with a box of tissues.

"Merta?"

She pushed her glasses up her nose and turned, her red eyes magnified behind her glasses. "Yes, Mr. Cooper?"

"What's wrong?"

She opened her mouth but no words emerged.

"Well?"

New tears swelled in her eyes.

Ian's patience snapped. "Speak, woman. I don't have all day."

She burst into tears.

Ian took a deep breath then turned to Nelson. "What happened?"

"After being offered one of Merta's cookies Ms. Duvall said her cookies were a health hazard and that she should be reported to poison control and listed as a possible risk."

Ian nodded. Unfortunately, she was right. He'd heard about Merta's cookies and his office staff fled when she brought in her latest culinary experiments: pudding with cornstarch, oatmeal-relish cookies and one of her favorites, pickle-banana bread. Of course no one was ever brazen enough to say anything to her face.

Ian shook his head. "It's just her opinion, Merta. It shouldn't bring you to tears."

She sniffed and lifted her watery gaze to his face. "Do you like my cookies?"

"I don't think I've ever had one."

"But you must have," she insisted. "Every month I prepare a special batch for you. I give them to Nelson to hand to you."

Ian glanced at Nelson who averted his gaze. He

knew Nelson had probably disposed of them long before they reached his desk. "Oh yes, those."

"Would you like one now?" She leaped up from the chair and shoved a tray crowded with brown lumps in front of him.

Ian took one then glanced up and saw Nelson standing behind Merta, vigorously shaking his head then wrapping his hands around his neck and miming a gagging reflex. "I'll save this for later. Now wipe your eyes and get back to work."

She smiled and left.

Ian lifted the lump to his nose and sniffed. "This smells like—"

"And tastes like it, too," Nelson added.

Ian wrapped it in a napkin. "I'll give it to Candy instead." As he was about to return to his office, he spotted another employee, Leonard Mills, cleaning out the coffeepot. His tie was tossed over his shoulder, his shirt disheveled and his sleeves rolled up. "What are you doing?"

"Remaking the coffee," Leonard said, vigorously rinsing the pot out. "Ms. Duvall said it didn't taste fresh."

"Who makes the coffee here?"

"I do. I make a fresh pot every morning."

"It's still morning. Why are you making another one?"

"Because she said it didn't taste fresh."

"And you agree with her?"

Leonard hesitated. "No, but—"

"Then why are you making a new pot?"

"Because of the *way* she said it."

"But she doesn't work here and I'm not paying you to make coffee."

"She can be very forceful."

"Then tell her to make it herself."

He shivered. "I'd rather make more coffee."

Ian glanced toward the office, then walked briskly over to the display where Mariella was instructing Serita Brickman, a recent hire in a peasant blouse with a plastic daisy in her hair. "Put it back, Ms. Brickman," he said.

Serita sent a nervous glance at Mariella then looked at Ian. "But—"

Ian enunciated every word. "Put. It. Back."

Mariella turned and looked at him. "I don't think the way you have the display is correct. I thought it was best to have it this way." She continued adjusting the display. The office fell silent. No one moved.

Ian kept his gaze on Serita. "I'm glad you are diligent in your task, but leave things as they are unless I instruct you."

Mariella moved toward him. "Mr. Cooper—"

Ian continued to address Serita. "Don't let anything distract you from your task. Nelson will help you."

Mariella stepped in front of him. "Mr. Cooper, I am speaking to you."

Ian looked past her. "And when Ms. Duvall arrives, please let me know." He turned, then disappeared into his office.

Mariella stared at the closed door, stunned, but within seconds her surprise turned to mortification then rage. She'd never been ignored in her life! People always paid attention to her. *Always.* He had the arrogance to look right past her. Her. Mariella Duvall. Her rage almost became a tangible creature taking over her body, making her skin burn, her hands tremble and closing her throat against words. However, with superior effort she managed to keep her face composed.

Nelson's voice cracked when he spoke. "The coffee's almost done."

Mariella didn't hear him. She couldn't. Rage had deafened her and narrowed her vision. All she saw was the closed door. Nobody shut a door in her face and got away with it. Mariella adjusted her jacket and skirt and retrieved her taupe leather portfolio that was sitting in the lounge chair. She marched up to the door and turned the knob. It didn't move. He'd locked the door. That's when her rage became fury and she did something she'd never done before. She pounded on the door, and at the top of her lungs shouted, "Open up this instant! I will not be treated this way. Do you hear me?"

Silence followed.

She pounded the door again until her fist ached. "Now!"

When the door didn't open, Nelson gingerly approached her. "Can I make a suggestion?"

She spun around and glared at him. "No. You may not. I'm leaving. I will not stand being treated this way."

"Should I make another appointment?"

She paused then said in a low acid-laden voice, "Are you trying to be funny?"

"No, I just thought that after you'd calmed down…" His words trailed off as the fire in her eyes became an inferno.

"Calm down? Do you think I'm overreacting? Do you know who I am?"

"No, yes," he said, quickly backing away. "I mean…I just thought—"

"Don't think. Just get out of my way." She pushed past him and stormed out of the office into the hallway. Tears of anger blurred her vision. She'd come early, barely able to contain her excitement at getting the chance to work for such a prestigious magazine. She'd even written down a list of questions. She took that list out now and tore it into little pieces. She hated him. She never wanted to see him again. She didn't care how gifted or brilliant he was or what opportunity he could give her. She would never work with someone who could be so rude.

As she rode the elevator to the ground floor, tears continued to gather in her eyes hot and stinging, but she didn't let them fall. Ian Cooper would not have her weeping like a dejected lover. He meant nothing to her. She wished Jeremiah was still alive. He cherished her and understood her. He had never treated her this way. He had always loved seeing her, no matter what time of the day it was. He especially loved it when she would "surprise" him and turn up early to be with him.

For a moment she felt foolish. Why had she bothered to come in the first place? He probably thought she was one of his father's women, and wanted to show her up. She wished she had never come. This was only the second time in her life that someone had ignored her in this manner. The first had been her now brother-in-law Alex.

Following the death of both of her parents, she and her three sisters had found themselves nearly bankrupt, and had to sell their family home. Luckily, a former friend of the family, Alex Carlton, who was now extremely rich, bought the house. Thanks to her quick thinking Mariella and her sisters had devised a plan to get him to marry one of them, allowing them to keep the house and not face financial ruin. While she hadn't displayed any open attraction to Alex, nor did she particularly have any feelings toward him, she had been his first, but not final choice.

It hadn't really bothered her, but for a brief period, one hour to be exact, she felt some of the same emotions she was now feeling, of being "passed over." She had never shared this with any of her sisters. When you're beautiful people rarely treat you as though you have feelings that can be hurt. So she pretended that she didn't have any. Ian Cooper had made her look foolish. She thought of the care she had taken to look good for the interview. It was all a waste. He hadn't even noticed her.

Mariella did not bother to sign out at the front desk; she did not want to spend another minute in the building. She stalked outside, into the bright day and glanced around for a taxi and was ready to signal one when her cell phone rang. She glanced at the number and saw that it was her sister Isabella who lived in upstate New York. Mariella considered ignoring it because she didn't feel like talking, then decided that at least she would be able to share with someone how horrible Ian Cooper was. She moved to the side of the building, shading herself from the glare of the sun.

"Hello, Izzy," she said. She searched her bag for her sunglasses and put them on.

"Hi, I just wanted to see how you're doing."

Her sister's voice was instantly comforting and her kind words made the dam break and tears fell behind the shade of her sunglasses as her anger spilled forth. She told her sister how awful Ian had been and how furious she was. Mariella was totally unaware of people looking at her. And for the first time, she didn't care and didn't try to put on a face.

Once Mariella stopped talking, her sister simply said, "Of course you're going back."

Initially Mariella couldn't speak. "Go back?" she repeated. "I'll never go back. He treated me terribly, Izzy." She rested a hand on her chest. "Me."

"I know," Isabella said in her usual gentle way. "But I've never known you to leave without a fight. Besides, this may be the break you've been looking for. His being rude to you isn't the worst thing in the world. It's happened to you before."

It might not seem to be a big thing to Izzy, but it was to her. Ian Cooper had ignored her. No, he had humiliated her. Getting attention was what she did. It was who she was. His actions had embarrassed her and she despised how ordinary and unimportant he had made her feel.

"What would Jeremiah say?" Isabella said.

"I don't care. He's not Jeremiah."

"How about Dad?"

Mariella looked at a passing cyclist.

"Mariella?"

"I'm still here."

"Just think. Are you sure it was that bad?"

Mariella gasped, outraged. "Do you think I'm making this up?"

"No, it's just sometimes…" Her words died away.

"Sometimes what?"

"You tend to overdramatize things."

Mariella stamped her foot, catching the attention of passing pedestrians. "I do not!"

"It's just that there may have been a reason for his behavior."

"There is a reason. He's a barbarian. I can't believe you're defending him. I'm hanging up."

"No, you're not. You're going to think about this rationally."

Mariella rested a hand on her hip. "Fine."

"I've never known you to run from a challenge, much less letting someone ignore you without letting them know how you feel. Mariella, you've never run from something you want."

"I'm not running," she said, insulted.

"Then why aren't you in his office? Go back and find out what he wants. If you leave, he wins."

She couldn't allow that. Izzy was right. He wouldn't force her to flee. She never fled a challenge. She quickly said goodbye to her sister, returned her mobile to her leather bag then marched back inside. In the elevator, she touched up her makeup, added more color to her lips, and adjusted any stray hair that had been misplaced by the wind.

"He's still in his office," Nelson said, jumping up from behind his desk when she entered the room.

"I know." Mariella sat. She would see him if she had to wait all day. She intended to meet with him, dog his steps, stalk him if she had to. He wouldn't get the chance to ignore her again.

Tense energy swept the office as Mariella waited. Time seemed to tick by slowly. Mariella didn't move. She didn't fidget or itch or tap her foot. She sat like a statue. At last, after an agonizing five minutes, the clock struck eleven. At exactly that moment the door opened and Ian stepped out. Everyone sent furtive glances at the pair, fearing something catastrophic was about to happen.

Ian looked at her and smiled. "Ms. Duvall, so glad you could make it." He held out his hand. When she didn't move to shake it, he reached down and seized hers. "Thank you for being so prompt." He pulled her to her feet in an effortless tug. "Please come in." He gently but effectively pushed her through the door then closed it behind him. He pulled out a chair and motioned to her to take a seat. She remained standing. Ian walked to his desk and sat.

Mariella studied him trying to use a dispassionate eye, but failing. No one could look at Ian Cooper dispassionately. His very nature made that impossible. He hadn't changed from the man she had seen the day before. Why would he? What had she expected? Why did it matter? Somehow from reading his biography online and looking at the pictures he'd captured, she'd expected him to be somehow different. She'd expected to see something gentle behind the arrogant features and devilish eyes. But that wasn't so.

She could see his eyes now and they completed her image of him, like a photograph being developed in a darkroom. He had a classically handsome face with compelling dark brown eyes, like a Benin sculpture. A very attractive man that would have Adonis weep with envy. She hated him even more. She tried to see him in three different ways. One as the talented photojournalist with a trained eye. Yes, now she could see his eyes as dark and compelling as his photographs. Then she tried to see him as a businessman running a successful magazine, which explained the arrogance that seemed to float around him. Lastly, she tried to see him just as a man, but she couldn't put that image together. He was an enigma. The photojournalist and businessman she could capture, but the *man* proved elusive.

Mariella stood in the middle of the room determined to put him in his place. "I am furious."

"Why?"

"First, I will not be manhandled."

"Manhandled?" he said, confused.

"You forced me in here."

"Did I? I thought you wanted to see me."

"I did."

"I usually meet my visitors in my office."

"Yes, but I will come into a room when I want to and—"

"So you have," he said.

"You're not making sense." Mariella could feel her temper beginning to rise again. He was toying with her.

"Of course I am. You're the one who's not. You say you want to see me in my office and here you are yet you're furious."

"I'm furious that you ignored me."

"But I just said 'Hello' to you."

"You said hello to me now, but not before."

"Before what?"

"Before *now*. I was here nearly an hour ago and you didn't even look at me."

"Impossible. How could I have seen you when you weren't here an hour ago?"

Mariella stomped her foot. "But I was here."

"No, you couldn't have been."

"I said I was." Mariella took a deep steadying breath, taking hold of her temper. She knew he was playing a game and she meant to win it.

"Ms. Duvall, there's no need to shout."

She raised her voice even more. "I will shout at someone who appears to be clearly hard of hearing. I was here nearly an hour ago."

"But you weren't here," he calmly replied. "What would you be doing here an hour ago?" Ian rested back in his chair waiting for her next response.

She leaned on his desk. "Waiting to see you."

He frowned. "Why?"

"Because I wanted to see you then."

"But I didn't have an appointment with you until now. Don't confuse yourself, Ms. Duvall. I'm sure you wouldn't have come an hour early for an appointment when you have better things to occupy your time. I know you are a considerate woman so you wouldn't have so arrogantly assumed that I would have seen you earlier than the time agreed. Your schedule must be so full that you're confusing me with someone else." He smoothly changed the subject before she could reply. "Mother, this is Mariella Duvall. Ms. Duvall, my mother."

Mariella started. She hadn't even noticed that there was anybody else in the room, much less a well-dressed attractive older woman, a toy Chihuahua and a large black Labrador.

"A pleasure," Shirley said, offering a tentative smile.

Mariella didn't return the expression. "I offer

you my condolences. It seems that your son is unfortunately in the early stages of dementia."

Shirley blinked, casting a wary glance at Ian.

Ian merely smiled. "Considerate and she has a wonderful sense of humor."

Shirley's gaze darted between the two. She didn't know how to reply.

Mariella stared at him, the level of her contempt evident in her voice. "You're—"

Ian interrupted her. "Let's get down to business. Please take a seat."

Mariella folded her arms. "I prefer to stand."

Ian stood. "Of course. Forgive me. I forgot to take into account your delicate sensibilities. That chair won't do." Ian came from behind his desk and pulled up another chair then pushed it into the back of Mariella's legs, forcing her to sit. "There, that's better." He glanced at his mother who looked as though she wanted to leave but knew of no way to exit. She shifted her body, looking out the window while stroking Candy, who lay fast asleep on her lap.

Mariella glared up at him and started to rise.

He rested a hand on her shoulder that felt like a vise and kept her in place, but his tone remained courteous. "No, don't get up. If you need something just tell me and I'll get it for you."

When she opened her mouth to reply, he turned and went back to his desk. "Good. Now that we're

both comfortable, I have a question for you.
You've taken pictures of celebrities and even had
Look Out magazine approach you. Why did you
turn them down?"

Mariella stared at him. How did he know this?

Ian clasped his hands together behind his head.
"Take your time. I have all day. I wouldn't want
to rush you. We all can't be quick thinkers."

I'll get you for that one. "I like to work for
myself," she replied calmly. All feelings of irritation, carefully tucked away.

"It would have been nice on your résumé."

"I already have enough impressive qualifica-
tions on my résumé."

Ian let his hands fall and leaned forward on his
desk. "Not impressive enough, but I admit you
have an eye." He sat back. "Let me tell you why
I asked you to come. We are looking for a photographer to complete the second part of my father's
last project. It is a photo layout displaying East
Coast seasons in a creative way. He had completed the photographs of the West Coast last year
and planned to do the East Coast this year. He
completed summer and spring. It was my father's
expressed wish that you complete fall and winter
for him. He was impressed with your work. It will
be an exclusive contract for six months to include
a full spread in the magazine and a gallery
showing."

It was too much. "You must be mistaken. I'm not good enough yet."

"He obviously thought you were."

"But what do you think?" She immediately regretted the question. She didn't care what he thought.

He flashed a cool smile. "It doesn't matter what I think. It's what he stated in his will. I agreed to follow his wishes."

"But you—"

"The reasons why I agree are immaterial. We both know that a project of this magnitude, with the publicity you'll gain from our magazine, will launch your career."

"And I'll be working with you?"

"*For* me. Yes. So what do you think?" He shook his head. "Never mind. I already know."

She looked at him, incredulous. "You know what I think?"

"Yes."

She blinked. "You don't even know me."

"You knew my father. That tells me all I need to know."

"Then you don't know very much."

"Do you want the job?"

Mariella stood. "It is a fantastic opportunity."

He flashed a smug grin. "Once in a lifetime."

"Yes." She lifted up his gold-plated nameplate and studied it. "I'd be crazy to say no."

"Yes."

She set the nameplate down and glared at him. "Then I must be certifiably insane because I wouldn't work *with* you, *for* you, *beside* you, or *above* you for any money in the world. I find your behavior appalling not to mention insulting."

His smile fell. "Now wait—"

"You claim to know me, but I know you more. You've always gotten your way, spoken your opinion, bombarded people with your power, made quick judgments, all the while dazzling people with your handsome face."

Ian rose to his feet and leaned toward her. "Kind of like looking in a mirror, isn't it?" he said in a low silken voice.

"If the mirror were cracked." She grabbed her handbag and portfolio, and headed for the door, nearly tripping over Sylvester, who had decided to lie sideways near it.

"Move," she said.

The dog slowly rose and stretched then yawned. He glanced up at her and blinked, then trotted to Ian's side. Mariella swung the door open.

"I'll see you, say nine, Thursday for our first meeting," Ian called after her.

Mariella turned, looked at him with pure venom, then slammed the door.

Ian sat back and laughed.

"Ian," Shirley said, grasping the front of her chest as though experiencing heart palpitations. "I've never seen such a woman. It's hard to believe your father had anything to do with her, although he was never particular as long as they were beautiful. And she certainly is."

His good humor suddenly died, replaced by a pensive look. "Hmm."

She fell quiet, her gaze worried. "Ian, what are you up to?"

"What do you mean?"

"You have that look. You wanted her to leave, didn't you? Not that I blame you. She is obviously on something to behave that way."

"Mariella has never taken anything stronger than cold medicine and she's never been my father's lover."

"How do you know?"

"She told me so."

"And you believe her?" Shirley sniffed at her son's naiveté. "Don't you know that women make it an art to say the things men like to hear?"

"She didn't lie to me."

"But the rumors."

"Rumors mean nothing to me in the presence of facts."

"What facts?"

"You just met her." He gestured to the door. "Dad could never have handled her and Mariella

likes to be in control too much to take anything
that would make her lose it."

"But what about the will? You can't deny that
evidence."

"No, but I'm sure there's an explanation."

"When it comes to your father even an explanation isn't good enough." She shook her head. "I
can't see any man who would want that vain, ob-
noxious woman," she said, adjusting her hair. She
then applied yet another layer of brilliant red
lipstick. Candy, used to the goings-on between
Shirley and Ian, was resting peacefully at the end
of the sofa, trying to go to sleep.

"You're looking at one."

"Ian, you can't be serious. You plan to make her
your lover?"

He laughed. "No, of course not."

She smiled, relieved. "Thank God for that."

"I plan to make her my wife."

Chapter 5

Shirley gaped at him. "You shouldn't joke like that. Someone might take you seriously."

"I am serious."

"But you can't be. She's horrendous, beautiful yes, but the beauty will pale in a few years. You couldn't be in love with her. I know you too well. Is this a competition? Or are you more like your father than you'd care to admit?"

His brown eyes turned cold. "Do you want to have a place to stay tonight?"

"I didn't mean—"

"Then don't compare me to him-again."

Shirley was quiet a moment then said, "Not that

it could ever be serious with you. You've never stayed true to anyone, except…" She stopped. He didn't fill in the silence. He liked that she was uncomfortable. The Coopers didn't like to talk about his first wife. Cathleen was ten years older, coarse, raw and brilliant. A photojournalist who'd competed with the men. She was as plain as she was courageous. She'd taken him out of his placid world of beauty and shown him what life was like for others. He'd met her at college his freshman year when she'd been presented as a guest speaker. She'd approached him and taken his picture then said, "Let me introduce you to life" and he'd taken her up on her offer. It had been the best pickup line in his life.

He remembered working with her on photo assignments. He found himself meeting people with no running water or plumbing—not in some third world country but right here in the U.S. They had traveled the globe, on several occasions, and over time he soon felt comfortable with what others turned away from, what made others cringe. He liked dark alleys, smoke-filled bars and subsidized housing. Cathleen had introduced him to a side of himself he'd tried to hide. They'd only been married five years when on a trip to Gambia their lives had changed…no, he wouldn't let himself remember.

He glanced up and saw his mother's worried look. She hadn't even tried to like Cathleen.

Both of his parents had thought he'd run off with her just to hurt them. As though he were some rebellious teenager, but it had been deeper than that, and he had vowed to never hurt like that again. Mariella was not Cathleen. That was why he knew she was perfect. He wanted her. He'd never be that vulnerable again, and with Mariella, he knew that wouldn't be possible. She thrilled and excited him. There was also a fresh vitality about her that he wanted to protect. He didn't know why, but he planned to find out. One thing he knew for certain—Mariella was the woman for him.

Gen let out a startled scream when Mariella stormed through the door of their condo.

"What happened?" she asked.

Mariella threw her purse on the dining table. "Ian Cooper."

"Didn't it go well?"

She tossed her portfolio on the couch. "No."

"What did he want?"

"He wanted to offer me an exclusive six-month contract to complete Jeremiah's project."

"You accepted, right?"

"I certainly did not," she said, offended by the suggestion. "I would never work with such a— well, I can't call him a man because he isn't one. He's a…a bastard completely impossible to be

around. Condescending, rude, utterly without
civility."

"But he's successful and could really help
your career."

"I don't need his help," she said through
clenched teeth. "Even if I did, I would rather hang
on to a broken branch over a fifty-foot cliff or
face falling into a sandpit than grab a hand he
offered."

"You're just upset."

Mariella raised her hands to the ceiling. "I'm
furious. I hate him."

"Think of your modeling career," Gen said
softly. "Didn't you have to work with people you
didn't like?"

"Not often." She flexed her fingers. "He kept
me waiting for over an hour."

"But Mariella, you did leave home rather early."

"He wasn't busy. He could have seen me."

"Sometimes, Mariella, you have to compro-
mise. I know you're not used to doing that,
but—"

"This man doesn't know the meaning of the
word. I'm sick of talking about him." Mariella
kicked off her shoes, and went to open her portfolio. She noticed two glasses on the side coffee
table. "You've had a visitor."

Gen suddenly looked shy. "Josh came by."

"I see. Don't let him monopolize your time.

You should see other men. You might get attached too easily. It isn't that way for men."

"I want to see Josh."

"The Cooper men are sly."

"Josh isn't like Ian."

"No, but he falls prey to Ian's influence. You wouldn't want your life dominated by the opinions of someone else, would you?" Mariella said.

"No." She sighed. "There is no way it will work anyway."

"Why not?"

Gen sent her a glance. "You know. We talked about it. Remember?"

"Maybe Josh wouldn't mind," Mariella said, thinking that having a sister-in-law with Gen's past would be a stain on Ian's image in his mind.

"But Ian would and you just said Josh listens to him. Ian wouldn't want someone like me married into his family." She bit her lip. "But if you could persuade him—"

Mariella widened her eyes and rested a hand on her chest. "Do I look like a magician? I couldn't persuade that man to do anything." She waved a dismissive hand. "You wouldn't want him as a brother-in-law anyway."

Gen shook her head as Mariella sat down beside her. "I think you're making a big mistake. What is six months to a lifetime of success?"

"I've already said no and I couldn't go back." She felt some of her anger ebbing as she thought of the possibilities. "He would love to see me grovel and I'll never give him the satisfaction of seeing me do so."

"Well, I guess that's that."

"Yes," Mariella said with a twinge of regret. She then felt annoyed with herself. She'd done the right thing. Her mother had taught her and her sisters about the important things in life. Being born beautiful had its downsides, her mother had always said, and since Mariella was considered the most beautiful, her mother had taken much effort to indoctrinate her regarding how and when to use her natural given power.

Men like Ian liked to dominate and she would not be dominated by anyone no matter how much he could help her career. She'd seen what women, especially beautiful ones, had done to succeed. She'd seen models sleeping with flabby, lecherous men in order to secure a contract; marry controlling older men who kept them as prisoners in order to access their fortunes and live well. She, and her youngest sisters, Daniella and Gabriella had known from an early age that they had been blessed with good looks, and their mother had raised them well. Growing up, she remembered the lavish balls, and countless courting, by wealthy men, who wanted her as their showpiece. Unlike her two sisters, who had succumbed to love, she planned on avoiding it at all costs.

"Remember, Mariella," her mother had said, shortly before she died, her lyrical island voice now weak, "you are the most beautiful flower in my garden, don't let just anyone pick you. When the flower is plucked from the branch, at that moment, it begins to die. You have been blessed with incredible beauty, don't ever give it away. Keep it, and use it to get what you want, but never let it be taken from you."

Mariella took a moment to reflect. Unlike her sisters, she had always been given whatever she wanted, but there was something that she knew she lacked. Had the way her mother raised her made her different? Why was it that in spite of having the best dress, the very best of everything, at times she wondered, what would happen to her if her looks failed?

She'd once caught the way her brother-in-law, Alex, looked at Isabella. Lovely, small Isabella who couldn't hold a candle to her looks, had a man gazing at her in a way no man had ever looked at Mariella. Briefly a jealous pang had gripped her and then left. Isabella needed a look like that from one man, but Mariella could elicit the admiration and desire of many men. Men who'd wanted to own her, but never would.

Men still ruled society, but no one would rule over her.

"Mom, will you stop worrying?" Josh said that evening, trying to soothe Shirley, who'd called him in hysterics.

"How can I help it?" she wailed.

"I'm sure he was kidding."

"I wouldn't be in this state if I knew he was kidding. You know Ian. To think he would consider linking up with that woman."

"I'll handle it."

"How?"

"You'll see." Josh hung up the phone and stared at his father's papers. He'd been shifting through them over the last week. "I bet you think this is funny. I'd probably laugh if it were happening to someone else." But he knew that handling Mariella was no laughing matter. She had her addictive charms and he'd built up his immunity by watching her around his father, but obviously Ian hadn't had that opportunity.

She was a Venus flytrap. He needed to give his brother some protection. He searched through the papers hoping for some damaging proof that his father and Mariella had been more than friends. He didn't care what she claimed, the will was proof that there was something more, he just had to find it. "Come on, Dad. I know you have something." At that moment he saw something and smiled. "Eureka!"

However, he wasn't in the same high spirits early that Thursday morning.

Josh hated meetings. What he hated more were meetings with his brother. What he hated more than that were meetings with his brother when someone didn't show up. Josh knew better than to look around the conference room at the others, who tried not to squirm in their seats, in the silence with the ominous ticking clock in the background. He didn't glance at the clock or his brother; instead, he pretended to type on his laptop. He resisted the urge to say "I told you so," because he had. He had warned Ian not to be overconfident when it came to Mariella.

"She'll show up," Ian confidently told him only two days before in his office.

"But Mom said she stormed out of your office and you've admitted that she didn't sign anything," he said, hoping to force his brother to see reason. He wasn't sure when to tell him about the evidence he'd found against her. He'd use it as Plan B if his brother refused.

"She was just upset." Ian stroked the top of

Sylvester's head. "Once she's thought things over she'll come back."

"No," Josh said, grimly staring at Ian's smug companion. "She won't."

Ian clasped his hands together. Sylvester looked at both of them with hope, that maybe they'd acknowledge him and give him his afternoon treat, but when they didn't he rested his head back down on his crossed paws, resigned. "She stormed out of my office once and returned. She knows how much this contract means to her career. Trust me, she'll come."

"Look, she can't ruin this for us. Did you tell her everything?"

"No."

"Should I?"

"No. The less she knows the better. Don't worry. She'll come."

But she hadn't come and Josh knew she wouldn't.

"Where does she live?" Ian asked, his low voice piercing the quiet of the room.

Josh hit a key on his laptop, his mind racing for the right words to calm his brother's anger. "I think we need to use a different tactic with her."

Ian rested his palm on the table. "Where does she live?" he repeated in the same low voice, which could be both frightening and soothing at the same time.

"Perhaps you should buy her something or take her out to dinner. I can think of a few great places."

Ian slowly stood. "Josh." He walked over to his brother, closed the laptop and shot him a glance. "Where does she live?"

Josh gave him the address.

Ian looked at the rest of the group. "This meeting is over."

Everyone hastily gathered their things and scurried out of the room.

"I told you she would be difficult," Josh said, following his brother out of the conference room. "You can't—"

"I can handle her."

"She could destroy this project."

Ian spun around. "Are you suggesting that she's more powerful than I am?" he said, a deadly edge hardening his tone.

Josh halted then shook his head, realizing his blunder. "No, I didn't mean that. I just—"

"Then stop worrying. I underestimated her pride."

"You underestimated *her*."

"Relax. She'll show up next time."

"You haven't even gotten her to sign the contract."

"She'll sign it."

Josh followed Ian to the elevators. "Don't fall for her ploy. You even had Mom afraid that you were interested in Mariella. You know…as a woman," he said as though the idea was preposterous. "Fortunately, I know that you're not. I know that it's just a strategy."

Ian pushed the Down button.

"It *is* just a strategy, isn't it?" he said, now unsure.

"No," Ian said softly, staring at the elevator doors. "It's not."

"What?" Josh jumped in front of him and waved his hands in his face. "Are you out of your mind?" Ian moved to the side and pushed the button again. "She's dangerous, not to mention she was Dad's lover."

"She said that she wasn't."

"She might say it, but—"

"But what?" Ian challenged. "You think she's lying?"

"Dad never had just female friends. I saw how he looked at her."

"So?"

"I saw how she looked at him."

"Yes?"

"And I found pictures."

Ian paused, then said, "How convenient."

"You don't believe me?"

"I believe you found pictures, but they're probably doctored."

Josh pulled out the pictures determined to prove his brother wrong. "That's not doctored."

Ian looked down at the series of photographs of Mariella in intimate lingerie in Jeremiah's bedroom.

"That's evidence," Josh said tapping one very convincing picture. "Don't get involved with her. I want this project to work." He shook his head. "No, I want this project to *end,* but first we have to get it started." He sighed. "I know we haven't always seen eye-to-eye, but trust me on this. I know Mariella more than you do. She's manipulative, vain and spoiled. The behavior she displayed today by not arriving, is just the tip of the iceberg."

The elevator doors opened and Ian stepped inside then turned to Josh. "That's fine," he said. "because I know how ice melts."

Chapter 6

Mariella didn't like mornings. Especially mornings when she woke up to the sound of someone pounding on her front door. She knew it couldn't be Gen, she had her own key, and besides, she had left early that morning to attend an appointment at the unearthly hour of 8:00 a.m.! The pounding continued. Mariella slowly grabbed her pink silk robe, removed her headscarf, slipped on her fur-lined slippers and walked toward the front door. Too irritated to look through the peep-hole, she opened the door with a force strong enough to knock someone over.

"What is it?" she demanded.

Ian stood there with his arms folded. "You lied to me."

She hardly heard the words. They were spoken so softly they could have been a whisper, but the hard edge to his tone made that distinction impossible. She'd seen him annoyed, playful, even smug, but never angry. He looked dangerous angry. Her dark puma looked ready to rip her to shreds. A knot formed in her stomach, but she refused to be afraid. "About what?" She tied the sash of her robe and saw his gaze dip to her figure with deliberate appraisal as though he'd reached out and stroked her. But the appraisal was quick and his heated gaze soon returned to her face.

"You lied about your relationship with my father."

Her fingers continued to fumble with the sash. "No, I didn't."

"Then what are these?" He held up the pictures.

She took them and flipped through them, pretending they meant nothing to her even though each one felt like a gunshot to the chest. "None of your business. Goodbye." She went to close the door.

Ian put his foot strategically in between, stopping her with such speed and fierceness that for a moment a shiver of fear crept up her spine. "Don't toy with me, Duvall."

"If you want to come in just say so," she said

with an air of flippancy she hoped would defuse his anger. Mariella turned away unable to meet the heat of his gaze and tossed the pictures on the table as though they didn't matter to her. "Why should you care about these?"

"You know why."

She turned and studied him. "Yes," she said, drawing out the word. "I do, but somehow I thought you would be different. Silly me." She folded her arms. "So you're jealous. What do you expect me to do about that?"

"I expect you to explain."

"No."

"Right," he said with contempt. "Because there is nothing to explain."

Her arms fell to her side as anger heated her words. "Let me tell you something, I didn't lie. I don't lie and I'm not going to explain those pictures to you or anyone because I don't have to." She pointed a finger at him. "But let me tell you one thing. Your father didn't own me and neither do you. Now I want you to leave."

Ian walked over to the table and opened his briefcase. He pulled out the contract and held it out to her. "I will after you sign these."

Mariella looked at the papers as though they were rotted fish. "I thought I made myself clear—"

"I don't care how you feel about me. This isn't

about me. This is what Dad wanted." He raised a brow. "Doesn't that matter to you?"

"That's emotional blackmail."

"That's business. You can look it over." He rested the contract down and opened it to the third page showing the generous compensation.

She closed it. "I'm not that broke."

"So there's nothing I can do to convince you?"

She tapped her chin thoughtfully. "Have you ever considered jumping off a cliff?"

"I've done it. Three times. I took a course on gliding. You should try it." His mouth pulled into the hint of a smile. "I wouldn't mind being there to give you a nice push."

She glanced at the contract. "So who are you going to use now?"

"No one. The project won't get done."

"What?"

"That's what Dad said." He placed the contract in his briefcase and averted his gaze. "Either you finish it for him or it's left incomplete. For some strange reason he thought you would be honored to finish his last gift to the world. He'd hoped—"

"Please don't speak for your father, you didn't even know him."

Ian did not look up. He became so still that the air seemed to thin and Mariella thought she would stop breathing, but she managed to hold her ground determined to fight him. *Got you,* she thought. He would never have the benefit of victory over her. She sat on the table and glanced down at the papers in his briefcase.

"I knew Jeremiah," she said. "I loved him. I loved his work and I loved the gifts his photographs gave. He never told me about this project and wanting me to do it. I'm sure he would have mentioned it to me. We were very close. And not in the way you and everyone else thinks."

"So now you know what *I* think?"

Mariella ignored his comment. "I bet you made this story up because you want to use me, or get back at me for—"

His eyes caught and held hers. "Don't flatter yourself, Duvall. You may think you knew my father, but I can assure you there's a lot about him you don't know. He was good at making people think they were close when they weren't. He mentored you and did a satisfactory job, but you've still got a long way to go before you could consider yourself among the best.

"However, his will didn't ask for my opinion, nor was I given an option to hire the best. I like to work with professionals, not someone who might expect preferential treatment. There are thousands of excellent photographers who would like an opportunity like this, but you're willing to throw it all away because I won't bend over like the rest. And you talk about love, but I don't think you loved my father one bit, otherwise it wouldn't be so easy to walk away from a project like this."

"You don't know anything."

"I know that if he'd asked me—" He stopped and snapped his briefcase shut.

Suddenly she saw how the situation looked to him, how painful it would be to have your father choose someone else to fulfill his last request. "He was probably afraid to ask you," she said softly.

Ian shook his head. "My father wasn't afraid of anything."

"He was afraid of being forgotten."

"You wouldn't let that happen."

She held out her hand. "Give me the contract." He did and Mariella scanned it, asked a few pertinent questions then signed. When she glanced up she saw the satisfied look on Ian's face. A realization struck her. "Why you," she sputtered. "It was all an act."

"No, not all of it."

"I actually thought you had a heart."

"Be careful not to make that mistake again."

"I won't."

His gaze became serious. "And protect that soft heart of yours."

She jumped down from the table and turned to look directly at him.

"I think you'll enjoy this project."

She studied him a moment. "You talk about me, but what about you. Don't you care about this project?"

"No."

Her eyes widened in surprise. "Why? Don't you care about his legacy?"

"His legacy?" Ian sneered. "He already has a legacy. He made half of it in bedrooms and hotels across America. As if the world needs another bunch of self-serving pictures. He liked sharing the vision of his own arrogance."

Mariella stiffened, offended by the harshness of his tone. "Jeremiah's pictures touched people. They were beautiful."

"Of course," he said in a bland tone. "That immediately gives them value. You only like beautiful things."

"That's not true."

"Pictures should show us reality."

"Beauty *is* part of reality too. Not just the heartache and pain and ugliness you like to show."

"You sell lies and illusions. You make people want things they don't need. You make people want things to be different than what they are. Your pictures cause nothing but self-hatred."

"And yours preach the world's sorrow without offering any reprieve. What are your solutions? You are an observer, but what actions do you leave your reader to take? Don't get on the high moral road with me. Anyone who thinks suffering is the only reality is also showing an illusion."

Ian opened his mouth then stopped. "Let's not argue."

She nodded. "Fine."

"However, we have to come to an agreement."

"I think we already have. I care about this project and I expect to be able to make all the important decisions."

"That will not be possible. You see, since I am paying for this project the final decisions will be mine. You will need to follow my instructions."

"But Jeremiah selected me because he knew I would honor him by doing what he would want, unlike you—"

Ian held up a hand. "Let's begin with one agreement. I'm not interested in hearing your description of what my father would or would not have wanted. Do the project. I am in charge of the purse strings. The final word will be mine."

Mariella shrugged. "I will complete the project as Jeremiah would have wanted. And will do my best to also meet your requirements," she said not sounding as though she would try very hard.

Ian narrowed his gaze. "I'll make sure you do."

"At least we understand each other."

"Yes, now let's understand something else." He pulled her into his arms and kissed her.

Chapter 7

Mariella didn't want to enjoy it. In fact she told herself not to. She told herself to remain rigid, stiff and inflexible until he stopped. But he didn't stop and for a moment she indulged in the delicious taste of his lips and his warm, firm body pressed against hers. She could feel the heat of his fingers through her robe, wondering if they could melt the fabric away.

His lips insisted that she answer his kiss and she couldn't deny him that demand. She felt herself falling into an abyss of emotions she couldn't understand or control and vainly fought against them. She struggled to free herself. "What are you doing?"

His arms tightened around her. "Kissing you," he said, pressing his lips against her mouth once more. "Don't you know what a kiss is?"

She turned her face away. "I don't want this."

"Don't you?" he whispered. He kissed her cheek then her neck.

She shut her eyes trying to block out the thrill he sent through her. "You'll have to control your attraction to me if we're going to work together. Now let me go."

He couldn't obey her. He liked holding her close. It was the only way he could be certain that she felt as he did. She could not put on her ice princess act when she was in his arms. He saw Mariella's beauty up close. Her smooth skin had felt warm and soft beneath his kiss. And the brilliance of her large black-brown eyes and silken lashes came through. She was more than beautiful, she was delicious. Like a French pastry—exquisite to look at and even better to taste.

"Are you finished?"

"Almost." He kissed her forehead then released her. "I'll control myself, but can you do the same?"

"What?"

"Are you going to lie and say you don't feel anything between us?" He snapped his fingers. "Oh, that's right. You don't lie."

Mariella turned away and went into the kitchen.

Ian laughed. "Do I make you uncomfortable?"

"You irritate me." She poured herself a drink.

He reached for the glass. "You shouldn't have."

She slapped his hand away. "I didn't." She lifted the glass and took a sip, her brown eyes meeting his over the rim. "If you're thirsty you can pour your own drink."

He rested a hand on the cabinet behind her. "I prefer what I see in front of me."

She took another sip, her gaze never wavering from his. "You don't scare me."

He let his finger trail up the glass. "I'm not trying to scare you."

"Then what are you trying to do?"

"Do you want me to tell you or show you?"

"I want you to leave."

"I'll leave once you explain those pictures."

She took another sip then licked her lips.

His face changed, but not as she expected. There was a sensitivity in his gaze of a true artist staring at an object he admires. It was what she'd seen in his work, a depth of emotion Jeremiah never showed and she wasn't comfortable with it. Lust she could handle, but his gaze proved far more intimate, as though he was seeing a part of her she didn't want revealed.

Mariella set her glass down with a clatter. "I'm going to get changed."

"Can I watch?"

"No," she said, glad he was back to his glib humor.

"Why not?" He picked up her glass, finished its contents then set it down. "I've seen you in less."

Mariella stared at him, not sure what annoyed her more, how he made himself at home or the fact that his manner was so effortless. "That was different."

"How? Did they do a lot of airbrush or was the body not yours?"

She walked away.

"I forgot," he called after her. "You're not getting paid."

She halted, halfway past the living room, then slowly turned. "You don't like models, do you?" she said, now certain that the look she'd seen in his eyes earlier had been her imagination.

Ian rested his hand on the wall and shrugged. "Not as a general rule."

"Why not?"

"You're basically irrelevant."

"I see." She rested a hand on her hip and cocked her head to the side. "Could I ask you a question?"

He stared at her, cautious. "It's not like you to ask permission."

"It's a personal question."

"Go ahead."

In an instant, her face and body posture altered as though a goddess had suddenly inhabited her.

Her skin seemed to glow, her face even more engaging than usual and for a second Ian wasn't sure he wanted her to ask him a question. Her brown seductive eyes reached him across the room as did the sudden low huskiness of her voice. "Do you know what Desire is?" He swallowed as her fingers toyed with the sash of her robe while she walked toward him with a slow easy gait that emphasized the tantalizing sway of her hips. "Desire is longing. Desire is needing. Desire is wanting." She stopped in front of him close enough for him to smell the lavender lotion she'd used earlier. "Do you have Desire?"

He had more than desire. If he wasn't careful his pants would unzip themselves.

Fortunately, Mariella folded her arms, breaking the spell, her eyes bright with triumph. "How much do you think that was worth?"

He grinned. "Duvall, I'd buy whatever you were selling."

"Good. So long as you know *I'm* not for sale." She touched the tip of his nose. "And if I were, you wouldn't be able to afford me."

He grasped her wrist, his palm hot against her skin. "But my father could?"

She pulled her wrist free, her face falling with disappointment. "You don't understand anything."

"Then tell me. I'm really bad at reading minds."

She shook her head.

"What's the price of admission? I'm willing to pay. We'd have fun together."

"There's more to life than money."

"I know."

It was his tone rather than his words that caused her to stop and really look at him. There was a sincerity that she hadn't sensed before, as though he'd revealed a layer of himself that he'd only allowed in his pictures.

"You look surprised," he said, amused.

"You are confusing."

"Or you're just confused." He shoved a hand in his pocket. "You're not the only person that people take at face value."

"How come your pictures are so dark?"

"Because that's how I see life."

"But your life is…"

"Perfect?" he finished. "Where did you read that?"

"I didn't have to read it. I can see it. You don't want for anything. You know you're incredibly handsome, well educated and financially successful and have the resources to do whatever you want to in life. You have a booming business and work with your family. Yes, I'd say your life is perfect. Are you actually going to tell me that it's not?"

"No."

She paused then said, "But then I could be wrong."

He stared at her for a long moment, his gaze cautious but at the same time curious. The expression didn't last. He glanced away placing a barrier between them. "You have a nice place." He pointed down the hall. "Is that your bedroom?"

"Don't you go in there!" she demanded as he walked past her.

He halted in the doorway and stared inside. "Son of a—"

She stopped before she collided with him. "What is wrong with you?"

He pointed to the series of three photos on the wall above her bed. "Where did you get those?"

"Jeremiah gave them to me," she said, unsure of the edge in his tone.

"Damn it, I told him to get rid of those."

"Why?"

He spun away. "Because they're mine."

Mariella stared at the images in horror. "But they can't be." She followed him down the corridor. "They're not your style."

He stopped and looked at her. "Yes, well that was me before—" He shook his head.

"Before what?" she pressed.

"Let's not shatter any illusions today. I have the perfect life and you…" He picked up the photos on the table and waved them in front of her. "And you are just an innocent woman mistaken as my father's mistress." He tossed the pictures down, then barged out the front door and closed it.

Mariella stood staring at the door. This was the second time he'd shut a door in her face and she didn't like it the second time around, any more than the first. She flung open the door, but he'd already gone. She slammed the door closed then kicked it. He was so aggravating. She didn't care what he thought of her. She didn't care if he didn't believe her; he wasn't any different than most people who always thought the worst of her.

Mariella went back into her bedroom and took down the photographs he'd claimed were his. She didn't want any part of Ian Cooper in the privacy of her bedroom. She brushed off some dust that had accumulated on the frames, and stacked them on her kitchen table. She had to give them away. She laid them side by side. Jeremiah hadn't told her they were his, but she'd just assumed they were because they were in his style.

How had the photographer of these changed so much?

And why had the sight of the delicate, joyful scenes caused him pain? That was the brief emotion she'd seen on his face before anger replaced it.

Did he feel a sense of betrayal? She could understand that. She'd felt it the moment Ian had shown her the photographs of her in Jeremiah's bedroom. He had promised her that he'd burn them. But she was beginning not to trust anything he had said. She'd wanted to give a dying man some pleasure, fulfill a fantasy, but that wish seemed silly now.

Nothing had happened between them. Yes, she'd allowed him to kiss her, but it had never gone beyond that. It was just a night of make-believe. Cast now in the cruel daylight, it looked sordid and cheap and that was how she felt. That was probably how Ian saw her. She didn't care. She began to tear up the pictures. Damn Jeremiah. She jumped when someone knocked—no, pound-ed—on the door. She gathered herself together and answered. She nearly fell apart again when she saw Ian standing there.

"I forgot my briefcase," he said gruffly, push-ing past her.

She grabbed the framed pictures. "You forgot these too."

He took the photographs, opened his briefcase and tossed them inside.

Mariella winced from the lack of care in which he handled them. "Please don't throw them away," she said as he snapped the briefcase shut.

He paused. "Why not?"

"Just don't."

He tapped the handle of his briefcase but didn't move.

The puma image came back to her. In his dark clothing he was a violent contrast to her light décor. He didn't just walk, he prowled, except now—when the air around him seemed as motionless as he was and she couldn't guess what his next move would be. He would make an intriguing study, yet she couldn't imagine taking his picture. He was too vibrant, too real to allow anyone to capture him in such an ordinary two-dimensional form. A part of her wanted to run, knowing that it would be a wise decision to put as much distance between herself and this man as possible, but another part wanted to stay by his side. She didn't move as though if she did he would vanish.

Mariella swallowed, taking the risk anyway. "If you are going to throw them away, you might as well give them back to me."

He raised a brow. "Are you going to hang them back up even though you know they're an Ian Cooper original?" he said, but there was a huskiness in his tone that hadn't been there before. It was rolling, deep with a hint of danger like the darkest jungle and wild thoughts entered her mind although her words were innocent.

"No, I'm going to hang them up trying to forget that."

His eyes dipped to her mouth. "Do you think you can?"

She licked her lips, her mouth suddenly dry.

The heat of his body reached out to her, and she fought the urge to move closer. "Can what?"

He raised his penetrating gaze to her face. She felt even more like prey. "Forget me." He opened the briefcase and handed back the framed photos. His fingers brushed hers, by accident or design it didn't matter—it had the same effect. All her senses came alert and she was suddenly painfully aware that they were alone and that anything could happen and that she wouldn't stop it although she knew she should.

She gripped the framed pictures to her chest. "Yes," she whispered.

Ian's gaze left her face and landed on the photos of her on the table. Although his expression didn't change, how he felt about her was clear. She could see him judging and condemning her, but when his gaze returned to her face demanding an explanation she boldly stared back refusing him one. The tension between them continued to escalate and she gripped the photos until she feared that the glass in them would shatter. But she still didn't move because she knew that as much as he angered her, she wanted him. She wanted to have him crush her body to his once more; she wanted those delectable demanding lips on hers. She wanted those dark eyes to strip her bare layer by layer then she wanted his hands to do the same. Her body tingled at just the thought, but Ian broke the spell by turning away and snapping his brief-case closed as though closing any possibility of a relationship between them as well. "I'll call you to set up a meeting."

She nodded and set the framed pictures down.

For a moment, Ian looked at her then without warning pulled her roughly into his arms. "Dammit, right now I don't care if you were his," he growled. "I will later, but not now." Then his hungry mouth was on hers smothering her lips with a savage mastery that sent bouts of ecstasy through her. He held her close against his hard body and the warmth that radiated from him felt like an inferno. Every part of her grew moist with anticipation and wanting. "I dare you to forget me," he whispered, his breath hot against her neck. They fell back on the table, Ian trapping her between his arms. "No, you won't forget this." He pushed back her robe to reveal her shoulders and pressed his lips to her bare flesh. He then kissed his way down her chest, then darted the moist tip of his tongue in the crevice between her breasts.

She arched toward him, lifting his shirt up so she could explore him as he explored her. He raised his head, his eyes bright with triumph, but they soon darkened again and he squeezed his eyes shut. "I can't," he ground out. "All I see is you and—" He pushed himself away and Mariella became painfully aware of the damaging photos that lay on the table beside her. She sat up, grabbing her robe tight around her.

Ian pressed his fists to his eyes, his voice raw with torment. "God, why him?" He let his hands fall then said in a flat dejected tone, "Forget it, I know why."

"Ian."

He stepped back and waved his hands as though warding off evil. "Don't say anything. Right now I'm willing to believe any lie that you tell me."

"I don't lie."

He seized a picture and shook it in front of her. "Then tell me what the hell this is."

For once she wanted to explain, but didn't know how. "It's not what you think."

"Oh no?" He raised his brows, surprised. "Should I read what's on the back?"

Hot tears burned her eyes, but she refused to let them fall. "We were friends!" She scooped up the rest of the photos and threw them at him. They scattered like a deck of cards. "He was one of my best friends and he was dying and I wanted to make him happy, okay? That's all. He was supposed to destroy them, so he deceived us both." No longer able to meet his hard stare, Mariella fell to her knees and began to pick up the pictures, desperate for something to do.

"I want to believe you."

She stood. "No, you don't. Otherwise you would." She turned on her heel and left. A few moments later Ian heard a door slam. He took a step forward to follow her then swore and spun around. He grabbed his briefcase and yanked the front door open, then slammed it so forcefully behind him the bang echoed down the corridor.

Mariella relaxed when she heard the door close. He was gone. She was safe again. For a while at least. She fell back on the bed, trying to grasp the shift in her life. But lying back only reminded her of the position she'd been in only moments before. She quickly sat up, wrapping the robe tight, but it didn't help. Ian had left his invisible stamp on her and she knew it would be a while before it faded. But she couldn't allow him to distract her.

Jeremiah had offered her the chance of a bright and profitable future. But he'd left behind a puzzle and he should have known her well enough to know that she hated puzzles. Especially those in human form. However, she had a chance to launch a new career and she would finish what Jeremiah started and no one would get in her way—not even his son.

Ian loved the silence of his darkroom. Some liked music; he liked the absence of sound, except the movement of liquid in the developing tank. He moved quickly but competently. He knew accuracy was the key to his trade. He could disappear in the darkness; he loved courting the shadows in his work and in his life. He did some editing on the computer, but to him nothing could replace the times he had spent in solitude developing his own pictures. Being alone hanging negatives, knowing instinctively which images would meet the world and which would be forgotten, gave him a high he couldn't explain.

He used the room as a chance to get away from everything just as his dad had done. If his dad wasn't with a lover, the darkroom was his other mistress. He'd let Josh and himself inside sometimes, and they'd sit quietly and watch him. It had been like magic at first. He'd seen how people looked at his dad and saw him as someone special but the "specialness" changed as Ian grew older, as stories of his father's life reached the papers, as he spent more time with more important people than with them. Over time they'd stopped being a suitable audience.

Now he didn't worry about that. No one could cast him aside. He liked the darkroom because he was in charge. He liked the ability to choose what to work on and what to discard. He liked to be in control. Things rarely surprised him in there, unlike real life.

Like the photos in Mariella's place. He wanted to remove the sight of them from his mind but couldn't. He'd been all around the world, dodging bullets and physical harm. He had a long scar on his side from a rebel who had attacked him because he hadn't wanted his photograph taken, that few knew about. After years of living out of a suitcase and always being where the action was he'd never thought that staying still could be just as dangerous.

He should have known that running always kept you only one step ahead of your past, staying still allowed it to catch up with you and it was assaulting him with a vengeance that surprised him. He'd thought age would have hampered the past, made it less vicious. He'd thought his father's death would have buried old pains, but they lingered and a few haunted him.

He shouldn't have agreed to take over the magazine, but it seemed fate had stepped in. He should have stayed away. He didn't belong here. He knew that and so did his father and yet when his father had asked him he'd said "Yes." He'd only seen his father twice in those years before he died. His father never asked for him and he'd never bothered to see his father. They never had much to say to each other and he wasn't good at pretense. Somehow it felt better that way. He didn't feel any regret. His father was never alone and likely had Mariella to fill his lonely nights. She was the type of woman who could make a man's nights very enjoyable.

He thought about her rendition of the Desire ad and his body responded just as fiercely as it had then. He swore. His father was a lucky SOB. Those pictures proved how lucky and they were a reminder for him to stay away. Dammit, he'd believed her once and she'd made him look like a fool when those pictures showed up. He couldn't risk believing her again no matter how genuine she sounded. No matter how much he wanted to. Mariella was right. He couldn't start an affair with his father's mistress. He had too much damn pride—pride that wouldn't allow him to trust her and be wrong again.

Ian left the darkroom and the realities of his life hit him. Sylvester, who had been waiting outside the door, rose to greet him. He heard his mother instructing his housekeeper, Lily, how to prepare Candy's special meals. He made a mental note to give Lily a raise. The phone rang. Ian knew who the caller was and waited for the third ring before answering.

"Otis, she won't speak to you yet. Give her space."

"At least let me—"

"I'll have her back to you in a few weeks as always."

"I know, but—"

"Stop calling every two hours, you're beginning to annoy me. Understand?"

"Yes," Otis said quickly. "I'm sorry." He hung up.

Ian returned the receiver then bypassed the living room and slipped into his study by a different staircase so that he wouldn't have to talk to his mother, but in his office he found his brother looking over papers.

"What do you want?" he said.

Josh glanced up from the papers. "You got her to sign the contract?" he said, stunned.

"Yes, I told you."

"You told me 'It's done' then hung up. How did it go?"

Ian sat behind his desk. "I just told you."

"No, you didn't. I know you got her to sign, but did she make any special demands?"

"She tried."

"What did she say about the pictures?"

"Said they were none of our business."

"I knew it."

Ian studied him then said, "Did you also know that Dad gave her my photographs?"

"What photographs?"

"You know the ones," he said quietly.

An acknowledgment of awareness came over his face. "No, I didn't know. It must have been more serious than we thought."

"She didn't even know they were mine."

"It was a harmless deception, he probably thought you'd never find out."

"Or perhaps he expected me to."

"How?"

"I don't know." He abruptly stood and walked into the family room adjacent to his office. He sank into a leather couch and Sylvester lay at his feet.

Josh sank into a chair facing him. "Maybe we're missing something."

"None of this makes sense. He forces me to use an inexperienced photographer to complete a major project, gives her my photographs and led everyone to believe that she was his mistress, and she denies she was ever one."

"It is weird," Josh agreed. "Why would she deny it? All the evidence points to the fact that she was. She didn't care what people assumed before. She's up to something and I think I know what it is."

"What?"

"She wants you."

Sylvester's growl interrupted Ian's reply. Both men looked up and saw Candy standing in the doorway wearing a purple bow and sequined jacket.

Ian pointed at the little dog. "No."

She made a little sound of protest, but Ian stared at her until she lay down, her head resting on her front paws.

Josh shook his head. "Why won't you let her come in? She's cute."

"She's ridiculous."

"That's not her fault."

Ian shrugged.

Josh rubbed his jaw thoughtfully. "She reminds me of Mariella."

"What do you mean?"

"She knows the Cooper with the power." Josh stood. "I'd be careful and keep my guard up around her." He passed by Candy and gave her a quick pat on the head then left.

Ian flipped on the TV, knowing that somehow Mariella had already penetrated his shield.

"Did you say thank you?" Gen said as she and Mariella sat in the living room with Ian's three photos on the coffee table.

"Did I say what?"

Gen sent her a look. "Mariella."

Mariella kept her voice neutral, while trying to erase what had happened earlier. "I was doing him a favor. He was just going to throw them away."

Gen lifted one eyebrow, surprised. "But they are so beautiful."

"I know."

"So you have to thank him."

"Why? They were a gift from Jeremiah."

"But now you know who they really belonged to. I think you should thank him in person."

Mariella stared at her. "Absolutely not. Do you know who we are talking about?"

"Yes, and while he is not one of my favorite people, it would be good manners."

"I'll send an e-mail."

"No, you'll send a card." Gen went to her room then came back with a decorated box with a wide selection to choose from. Mariella shifted through them, then picked up one showing a rainy scene.

"But that's dark," Gen protested.

"He likes dark."

"What are you going to say?"

"I'll think of something."

"Try to be polite."

Gen's idea wasn't bad. She'd thank him and send him a message too. A message he couldn't ignore.

She grinned. "Of course."

Chapter 8

A couple days later, Ian received a card at his office. He stared at it for a while because he wasn't used to receiving cards aside from the holidays. He knew from the return address that it was from Mariella. Her large, bold handwriting took up nearly half of the front of the envelope. Just as he was about to open it an important call came through and for the rest of the day work took precedence.

At home, a large basket of flowers arrived for his mother, who promptly wanted to get rid of them. She went on a tirade about men's oppressiveness; Sylvester nipped Candy for trying to eat

out of his bowl and then Shirley became hysteri-
cal although Candy was unharmed. Late that night
in his bedroom Ian finally had a chance to open
the card. He sat on the edge of his bed and tapped
the unopened envelope against his palm. What
game was Mariella up to?

He looked at Sylvester who lay curled up in his
bed. "What do you think this is?"

Sylvester yawned.

Ian nodded. "Yes, you're right. It's no big deal."
He opened the envelope and pulled out the card
and pieces of a picture fell to the floor. He
gathered it up, then read the note inside. "To illusions."

Ian smiled at the pieces in his hand, knowing full
well which picture it had been. So she was saying
that it was an illusion. It was a risky move on her
part; he didn't trust easily and he knew more about
why he had to hire her than she did. However, his
father had been a magician behind the lens. With
a trick of the light or the right angle he could show
what he wanted people to see, instead of what was
real. Ian weighed the pieces in his hand. "You win,
Duvall," he said with reluctant admiration.

Sylvester growled.

Ian didn't look up. "Candy, go away."

He heard a squeaky toy drop.

Ian glanced at her. "You have this entire house.
Why do you want to come here?"

She didn't move.

He dumped the pieces of the photo in the trash and walked over to Candy. She began to wiggle with excitement until she couldn't contain it anymore and began to jump up and down.

"Calm," he said.

She instantly sat still although her tail continued to wag wildly.

Ian bent down and took off a frilly night robe Shirley had put on her. "All right, come on." He stood and began to turn but she didn't move. She looked up at him and then the robe.

"I don't believe this. You want this?" He lifted up the robe and her tail wagged faster. "You are demented." He replaced the robe. "Now come on." He pointed at her. "And if you think I'm tucking you in, you might as well leave now." He tossed a fluffy dog pillow on the floor. "Go to sleep."

Candy began to walk toward Sylvester's bed, but he growled and she thought better of it and climbed onto the pillow. Ian picked up Mariella's card and tapped his chin. Josh didn't trust her, his mother thought she was crazy, but he didn't care. There was more to Mariella than anyone knew and he planned to find out.

The next couple of weeks everything moved quickly. Mariella met with Ian and Josh on several occasions to discuss and review the

details of the project. While not always in agreement, Mariella was not her usual self at the
meetings, which made both Josh and Ian a little
suspicious. She did not argue or emphasize her
point; instead, for the most part she remained
silent. What was she up to?

Once the specifics had been decided, the
schedule for the various photo shoots to include
Georgia and Vermont were finalized.

With only two days before having to fly to
Atlanta, Mariella and Gen's schedule was filled
with taking care of stopping their mail and paper
delivery, canceling their maid cleaning service
and rescheduling other appointments until after
the end of the project, which would not be finished
until winter. Gen made all the flight arrangements
while Mariella focused on the specifics of the
project, and gave requirements to Gen about the
models and assistants she would need on hand at
each location.

Josh was responsible for making all the final arrangements and after several run-ins with
Mariella, for his lack of paying attention to detail,
asked for Gen's help in meeting all of Mariella's
requirements.

The first assignment was scheduled in Atlanta,
Georgia. On a dreary overcast day with a hint of
rain in the skies in mid-autumn, Gen and Mariella
boarded a plane and arrived in Atlanta. When trav-

eling in public, which was always first class, Mariella was dressed incognito with a large-brim hat, dark glasses and a large shawl. While she was used to being recognized and gawked at, she was in no mood for uninvited fans coming up to her and asking for her autograph.

However, during their flight, their notoriety had not gone unnoticed, and even the pilot and co-pilot had personally introduced themselves. Once on the ground, they were greeted at the gate by the chauffeur of the limousine service Josh had engaged. He was a smartly dressed young man, holding up a sign that read Ms. M and Ms. G. Mariella, in her customary manner, pointed to the porter, coming up behind them pushing a large cart with their luggage and equipment.

At the hotel, Gen took care of the registration, while Mariella instructed several hotel bellboys to take her luggage and belongings to their room. Upon entering the suite, Mariella continued giving orders about which items needed to be put where and the care that must be taken with her photography equipment. Gen, on the other hand, was busy looking at the large gift basket that greeted them in the hallway. It was filled with an assortment of herbal teas, honey and honey dipper, pretzels, sesame crackers, smoked salmon, Camembert cheese spread and sweets.

"Mariella, look at this."

"I wonder why they're treating us this well."

"They have the money."

"That's not the point. Photographers don't usually get this kind of treatment."

Gen opened a sweet and popped it in her mouth. "Who cares? You should try one."

"Gen, I can't think of food right now. I need to freshen up." They had only half an hour to get settled in their room, before meeting with Josh. After changing into a more relaxed outfit, consisting of a cotton wrapped skirt and fitted T-shirt, Mariella rang the front desk to get the room number for Josh. While both suites were located in the private penthouse section of the hotel, Josh's suite was on the very top. As they exited the elevator, Gen said, "Mariella, will you need me this afternoon? I mean, I know what you're like when you are getting ready for a shoot. Besides, you will probably be busy and I was wondering…"

"You want to have some time with Josh." They approached the door and she knocked. "We'll see." Josh opened the door dressed for fun. He was wearing a caramel spun-cotton crew-neck short-sleeve top with matching khaki pants and leather loafers. He directed Gen and Mariella to a small study area off the living room.

"The view from here is fabulous," Gen said excitedly, as she looked out on the panoramic view his suite afforded. They could see some of

Atlanta's tallest buildings, mostly grouped in the downtown area including the Georgia World Congress Center, Georgia Dome, CNN Center, Centennial Olympic Park and the Atlanta Contemporary Art Center. "My, how the city has changed since we visited it last," Gen said.

"When was that?" Josh asked.

"A long time ago, when my dad brought us here for a visit."

"Can we get down to business?" Mariella said. "We're not here on vacation, or at least, I'm not."

Josh pulled out a large binder with all the specifics Mariella would need for the first shoot. True to her style, Gen knew that at this point, the best thing for her and Josh to do would be to leave Mariella to do what she needed. Mariella picked up the binder. "Do you have the contact information for the talent agency?"

"Yes," Josh said. "I've contacted the head of the agency, Donna, to let her know you will be contacting her today."

"I'll take these back to my suite." She looked directly at Josh. "Gen will be available later. Right now we have work to do." After briefly reviewing the specifications back in their hotel room, Gen and Mariella took a taxi to meet with the agency.

At the Donna Anderson Agency, Mariella and Gen waited in the office while Donna completed a prior schedule. Donna was a bulldoglike woman with frizzy brown hair and cat-shaped glasses known for being vicious with her remarks. She prided herself on her forthrightness. She was not an attractive woman, but she didn't have to be. She had power. When Mariella walked into her office she heard Donna shouting at a model.

"Why does Okolo Samit keep sending these cows to me? Have you looked at yourself? You have fat hanging all around your middle. Honey, get out of modeling and become an actor. They have things called 'cattle calls' and you'll fit right in."

The reed-thin girl raced past Mariella in tears.

"Do you have to be so harsh?" Gen asked.

Donna turned to her ready to give her a harsh reply then censored her words in case they were possible business contacts. "It's better to be harsh now than having her sit at home waiting for a photo shoot that will never happen. What do you want?"

"We're here about the *Flash* photo shoot," Gen said.

"Oh, yeah. I've got a few girls in mind."

"But we'd agreed to hold an open call," Mariella said.

"We'll do that too, maybe. Give me a few minutes then we'll get to business." She turned to her assistant. "Call in the next one."

Another girl entered with more confidence than the last.

Donna looked her over. "Her breasts are uneven. Get me someone symmetrical. I'm not trying to sell a Picasso painting." She pointed at the girl. "Get those fixed and I'll be able to use you. Next!"

Watching Donna brought back the harshness of the business for both Gen and Mariella. Being attractive wasn't enough. You had to be photogenic and have perfect bone structure. A job could fall through for no reason. You could be hot one moment and not the next. A world that showed such glamour had an underbelly of drug use, eating disorders, cold agents, money problems and fierce competition.

At last Donna had completed her strange weeding out process and sat down with Mariella and Gen at a small round table set off to the side.

"Heard you were dropped from Desire," she said to Mariella. "Anti-aging is still big. We could have you sell facial creams."

"I'm not interested."

"Probably best. Blacks don't sell anti-aging creams well." She turned to Gen. "It's like having you sell eye shadow," she said referring to Gen's nonexistent upper lid.

When Mariella opened her mouth to reply, Gen quickly rested her hand on her arm to stop her.

Donna continued talking. "You know if you considered surgery you might get your career back on track. Get those eyes widened and you could pass for say Native American or Latina. With your skin tone you could pass for a lot of things and that will work in your favor. I'm not making any promises, but you can think about it."

"Right," Gen said.

"We didn't come here as models," Mariella said, trying desperately to hold back what she really wanted to say.

Donna shrugged. "Hey, just in case the photography thing doesn't go as you plan, I'm just laying out some options."

"Well, I think your options—"

"Are something we'll think over," Gen finished, sending Mariella a pleading look.

"You do that," Donna said. "Now I'll take care of the hiring and paperwork. You can leave everything to me. You're just the photographer. I was hired to get the models for you." She smiled without warmth or sincerity. "Think of yourself as the technicians."

"Fire her," Mariella said to Josh as he finished his lunch.

Josh stared at her with his sandwich halfway to his mouth. "What?"

"You heard me. She has to go."

"Who?"

"Donna Anderson. I will not work with her. Is that clear?"

"But Ian said—"

"Then he'll have to work with her because I will not." She stormed away.

Josh lowered his sandwich, his appetite gone, then picked up the phone. He dialed Ian's number and when he picked up said, "You'd better get down here fast."

Chapter 9

The next day the puma struck at noon. He stalked his prey in the Magnolia Midlands in southeastern Georgia among the scent of honeysuckle and the sound of cranes landing on the lake's calm waters. His prey was unaware of his presence; the chaos of the shoot preoccupied her thoughts.

Mariella remembered her modeling days—scurrying here and there, impossible quick-outfit changes, endless arrays of hairstyles and makeup artists. But she wasn't the one on show this time. She was the photographer; the conductor of this orchestra. This was her time to shine and she did. The shoot went well.

After her final shot, she called it a day and then saw Ian in the distance. The shades were back, but she could feel the power of his gaze. Her heart foolishly started to beat faster. They'd been civil to each other since their last meeting in her condo. She'd been accommodating because she preferred to be out of his presence. Being near him did strange things to her and put unsettling thoughts in her mind. Those thoughts returned as he approached her. Briefly she imagined him grabbing her and placing his lips on hers. She knew what his lips tasted like and didn't mind another sample.

No, that wasn't true. She wanted more than a sample. She wanted a full out feast. She wanted to rip off his sunglasses and see his eyes darken with desire. She wanted to feel his touch and touch him in return. To *know*—not just imagine—the sculpted muscles under his clothes from his broad chest to his sturdy thighs. She cursed her wandering thoughts and steeled herself for his approach.

He stopped in front of her. "Glad that's over."

She glanced down and kicked the grass, wishing his nearness didn't affect her so acutely. "I wish it were over," she grumbled.

"What?"

She gathered her courage and looked at him.

"What are you doing here?" she demanded, staring at the twin mirror images of herself in his lenses.

"Supervising."

"Don't you have other projects to supervise?"

"I consider this my pet project."

"I thought you didn't like this project."

He lowered his tone. "Let's just say that there are certain parts of it that I find *very* attractive."

His voice brought a tingle of awareness to her skin. "I see." She lifted up her camera ready to take his picture. "Speaking of attractive…"

He put his hand over the lens. "No one takes a picture of me without my permission."

"But it's so tempting," she said, lowering the camera. "You'd make an excellent study. Except for your clothes."

"What's wrong with my clothes?"

"Are you aware that there are other colors besides black?"

He looked stunned. "When did that happen?"

She shook her head, but couldn't help a smile. "You only wear black although you'd look good in any color and you don't like your photo taken although you're very photogenic. Why do you only like to be behind the camera?"

"I'm shy." Before she could argue he said, "Josh tells me that we have a little problem."

She cleaned the lens of her camera. "We won't once you replace that woman."

"Donna?"

"Yes."

"And if I don't?"

She looked at him as though he'd just asked her to walk in front of a train. "But you will."

"Why should she be replaced?"

"Because she's unsuitable and she puts the girls down. I want her off the project." She lifted the camera and aimed it at something in the distance. "Either she goes or I do."

"You know I don't like threats."

"It's not a threat." She snapped the picture then lowered the camera and looked at him. "It's a statement of fact."

He bent his head and studied his hand. "Have you ever been sued?" he said quietly.

"What?"

He didn't raise his head or his voice. "You signed a contract. It would be a shame to break it."

"You wouldn't sue me."

"Would you like to find out?" He looked at her. "It will be an expensive mistake. I assure you."

"You don't even care about this project. Who cares if I stay on it or not?"

"I told you, if you don't do this project it doesn't get done. I don't like leaving things unfinished."

"You're being irrational. I can't work with her. She's arrogant and vicious."

"More vicious than you?" Ian suddenly smiled with interest. "Then I have to meet her."

* * *

Donna was everything that Mariella said and worse, but Ian kept his thoughts to himself, determined to stay with her. Donna was good at what she did and he wanted the best.

"Well?" Mariella demanded when she saw Ian in the hotel corridor as she exited her room.

"She stays."

"I see." Mariella turned.

"Going to your room to pack?"

She opened the door.

Ian followed her. "I wasn't bluffing about a lawsuit."

"And I wasn't bluffing about leaving." She stepped inside her room.

He held the door before she could close it. "I could destroy you."

She looked at him in challenge. "Really? People have tried and failed before. Do you think you're different?"

His eyes narrowed in warning. "Mariella."

"I will not work with her. And I certainly will not work with someone who approves of her." Mariella released her hold on the door.

Ian shut it behind him. "This is business. My personal feelings about her are immaterial."

Mariella walked over and sat on her sofa. "There are different ways to do business. This industry is hard enough without people putting you down. You don't know what it's like to be under a microscope. To constantly be judged. To have your worth based on five extra pounds or another candle on your birthday cake."

"Well, that's what this business is about and those that can't take it need to get out because it's not going to change because your feelings might get hurt."

"You don't care—"

"No, I don't," he cruelly interrupted. "I don't care because if the value of yourself is so tied up with how you look then you're already lost and there's nothing anyone can say to make that all right. You know how I feel about this industry. There are girls working in Burger King and Motel 6 who would love to get the chance to be models.

"But there are also people who are actually using their *brains* to develop and create things that will benefit humanity in some way." He threw up his hands. "So what if you don't get a chance to sell a piece of clothing? It's not the end of the world."

Tears of rage gathered behind her eyes, his words cutting deep. She leaped off the sofa. "I know that you think that we're useless sculptures that have no function. But let me tell you something. This face is my gift to the world. I still get letters from young girls who ask for my advice about beauty, yes, but also about life and I feel that in a small way I help them. Just as Jeremiah didn't ask for the gift of photography or Edison didn't ask for the gift of invention, we all use what gifts we can to make life better for others and I do that and so do others like me."

"You can snub your nose, but we humans live for beauty. We enjoy seeing beautiful things. This project is about the beauty of the seasons and beautiful women from different states. And it will sell. And it will make money for the ordinary person in the factory who would not have a job if this magazine didn't exist so that you can hire people to clean your house and keep your lawn pristine."

Ian blinked, unmoved. "So models actually help make the world go round?" he said blandly. "I never thought of it that way."

Mariella shook her head, frustrated. "If I didn't know you better, I'd think you actually felt guilty that you were attractive." She saw his face change and knew she was right. "That's it. You feel that you need to compensate by being foul." She walked into the kitchen. "I would ask why, but I really don't care."

Ian pounded on the counter. "But I want you to care!"

Mariella stared at him stunned. "What?"

He shook his head in regret and ran a hand down his face. "I didn't mean to say that."

"But you did say it," she said, not ready to let the subject drop.

He sighed, resigned. "I know."

"Why did you say that? What does it mean?"

"You know," he said softly.

"You want me to *care* about you?"

He smiled. "You can't imagine that, can you?" His smile grew at the astonished look on her face. "No, I can see you don't." He suddenly laughed. "You know we're going to find this really funny after we're married."

She took a hasty step back. "After we're what?"

"Married." He dismissed the topic with a wave of his hand. "But that's not the issue right now. Are you leaving?"

She raced into her bedroom. "I certainly am now." She grabbed her suitcase from the closet and placed it on her bed. "You must be insane. Married to you? Never."

Ian leaned in the doorway. "I really hate to see you leave. I was scheduled to have dinner tonight with Yolanda Stanton and her husband and had hoped to take you, but since you won't be here…"

Mariella froze. "You don't mean the owner of IMPULSE, the top end fashion magazine?"

He nodded. "Yes. They have a formal event coming up and are looking for a photographer. I told them about you and they would like to work with you once this project is over."

She sent him a suspicious look. "This is a bribe."

He grinned.

"I'll think about it."

"Don't think too long." He winked. "I'm picking you up at eight." He bowed then left.

Mariella sank into her bed. He was impossible. What did he mean after they were married? He wanted to *marry* her? It had to be a ploy to put her off balance. And his strategy worked. She actually thought about it. It wouldn't be a bad match. He was rich, handsome and powerful. The problem was she wouldn't be able to control him—that would take cunning. But with practice she could get used to his ways....

Mariella jumped to her feet. What was she thinking? She could *never* marry him. Ever. They'd argue all the time. It was out of the question. She pushed the thought from her mind and stared at her opened suitcase. It was cowardly to run away, however. Just because she hadn't gotten her way didn't mean she should walk away from a great opportunity. She could handle Donna. She would counter her cruel remarks with kinder ones. And she could handle Ian, too—with velvet gloves.

Ian arrived on time as expected. He frowned when he found Mariella still in her robe. "I'll be ready in a minute."

"You should be ready now."

She disappeared into her bedroom.

He sat down on the couch and stared out the window then picked up an old magazine and flipped through it. Then he saw Mariella's Desire ad. It was an old ad but the woman hadn't changed. Millions had wanted Desire, millions had wanted her. Some still did. Jealousy gripped him at the thought of all the men who had come before him, but he was secure in the fact that he would be the last. He called out to her, "If you're not ready in two minutes, I'm taking you as you are."

"I'm ready."

He glanced up and the magazine fell unnoticed from his fingers. It was as though the woman from the Desire ad had suddenly materialized in front of him. She wasn't a real woman, she was a dream— a fantasy. And this almost unearthly vision emerged from her room in an off-white, bare-back halter dress, with her hair smoothly pulled back and adorned with a mother-of-pearl hair comb. A hunger—dark, potent and fierce gripped him with a ferocity he couldn't control. He jumped to his feet aware of only one thing: he wanted her. *Now.* He glanced briefly at his watch before he walked toward her. He didn't have much time.

Mariella put on her shawl. "Okay, let's go."

Ian removed it with slow deliberation, the

material whispering against her skin as it slid away. "There's no need to rush."

She reached for the shawl. "But we don't want to be late."

He tossed the shawl on the coffee table. "We won't be late."

She folded her arms, unsure of his strange mood. "You sound very certain of that."

He unfolded them. "I am."

Her mouth widened into a smile. "Do you want to kiss me?"

He returned her smile. "No," he said, his large, warm hand skimming the length of her bare back until it reached her zipper. "A kiss won't do." He brought the zipper down with agonizing ease. Although his touch was light there was something fiercely possessive about the way he looked at her that called out to every feminine instinct in her. Mariella bit her lip; she had wanted to tempt him. She'd chosen the dress specifically, but she hadn't expected this. She hadn't expected his look or reaction to it.

"We don't have time," she said quickly.

His low voice was barely a whisper. "This won't take long."

She blinked. "Is that supposed to be romantic?"

He unhooked the latch around her neck. "If I had more time I'd be the most romantic man you'd ever met."

"I find that hard to believe."

"You're right, I'm lying." He pushed her dress from her shoulders and it fell to her feet. His hungry gaze exploring every curve of her body.

Mariella felt pleased by the survey as his gaze dropped to her black lace panties. But soon her pleasure turned to unease as the silence between them grew and Ian didn't make a move toward her. She opened her mouth, desperate to say something, but he pressed a finger to her lips and shook his head. "You don't need to say anything." He halted any attempt at protest and she didn't care. Her fingers unbuttoned his shirt and he took it off and tossed it aside. Her imagination hadn't done him justice. His sleek, hard body made her fingers ache for contact and when they did it wasn't enough. Soon she was in his arms, her skin prickled as his flesh met hers.

"I just thought of my own cologne," he whispered against her mouth.

"What?"

"Surrender."

"Is that what you want me to do?"

"No, I expect you to."

"You'll be disappointed. I don't surrender."

"You will."

He smothered her cutting reply with his mouth and effectively made her forget it. Their passion was primitive and raw and they enveloped each other with wild urgency. They fell against the wall, making two pictures swing precariously and nearly tipping over a vase. They didn't notice. They didn't notice the phone ringing from management or the knock on the door soon after from housekeeping, who had been summoned earlier by Mariella who'd requested extra towels. All they cared about was satisfying the desire they elicited in each other, of soothing a hunger that seemed insatiable. Mariella reached for his belt, then glanced at the wall clock and groaned. "Oh, God we're going to be late."

"We won't be late," Ian said through clenched teeth, the evidence of his desire pressing against her thigh.

"Yes, we will. Look at the time."

He buried his head in her neck. "I don't want to."

"You have to." She tried to push him away, but failed so she bit his shoulder. He glared at her; she stared back unmoved. "Ian, look at the time."

He glanced at his watch then swore.

"See?"

He slowly traced a circle around her nipple then raised his gaze to her face, his eyes full of deviltry. "We could cancel."

She grabbed his hand to stop his distracting activity. "That would be rude."

He lifted a sardonic brow. "Do I look like the kind of man who cares about being rude?"

"You said they wanted to see me. I want to make a good impression."

"You do." He bent to kiss her again. "I like you very much."

She turned her face away. "We need to go."

He hung his head. "Damn." He shut his eyes and rested the palm of his hand on the wall behind her. "I just need a moment."

She grinned, amused by his annoyance and wiggled against him. "You'll make us late."

He playfully traced his finger down her throat, but didn't smile. "Don't toy with me."

She stopped moving.

He removed his hand. "Thank you."

Mariella stepped away from him and quickly pulled on her dress. She watched him snatch up his shirt and angrily button it. She cleared her throat hoping to lighten his mood. "They're your friends."

"I'm beginning not to like them anymore," he grumbled, tucking in his shirt.

Mariella checked her image in the mirror then grabbed her shawl and handbag. "I wouldn't be in this dress if it weren't for them."

Ian stalked to the door and swung it open. "No, you'd be out of it," he growled then softened his statement with a wink.

Chapter 10

Over a half hour later, Ian and Mariella arrived at a grand house several miles outside of Atlanta. It was a stately new home with a classic colonial feel sitting on over six acres of land. The front exterior masonry was superb, with a retaining wall made out of gleaming rocks around the circumference of the house. Large double-hung thermopane windows provided ample lighting and elegance.

Inside a two-story foyer and center hall greeted them and the housekeeper showed them into the large family room furnished with black granite, wood-paneled gas fireplace and enormous windows.

The Stantons lived well, but had an easygoing manner that took Southern hospitality to another level. Though dressed in expensive designer clothes their greeting was anything but subdued. Mariella wondered how they could know Ian who looked and seemed so dark and brooding in his customary black. But they embraced him like relatives would and although Ian's reply was more tempered, it was clear that he was glad to see them.

Following a sumptuous five-course meal, they retired to the formal living room, an oversize room with a ten-foot vaulted ceiling, stone fireplace trimmed with Italian marble and gleaming wood flooring.

"So tell me how things are going?" Yolanda's husband Gregory asked, pouring each of them a glass of white wine.

"Well, Mariella is getting a handle on things," Ian said.

"Everything is perfect," Mariella countered.

The conversation soon turned to photography and became a lively discussion. Suddenly they heard the front door slam and loud voices.

"It's not fair!" a girl shouted. "Give it back!"

"No," another girl replied. "I bought it so it's mine."

"But I saw it first!"

"Girls!" Gregory called. "What is going on?"

Two girls about fifteen and seventeen appeared

in the doorway. The older girl was lanky with big
eyes and her hair in Nubian knots framing her
face. The younger girl had small slit eyes and a
round face with an impish grin. Her face was
framed by expertly woven cornrows ending in a
puffed ponytail on top of her head.

"Our daughters Hannah and Tatiana," Gregory
said as though embarrassed at having to make the
introduction. "Girls, say hello to our guests."

"Hello," they replied. Both girls instantly recognized Mariella. They were used to having famous
people including models, movie stars, diplomats
and others come to visit their parents and didn't
blink.

"Now what is going on?" Yolanda asked, agitated
fingers stroking her impeccably groomed hair.

The older one, Tatiana spoke up. "I saw a skirt
that I thought was great and I wanted to buy it, but
Hannah got to it first even though she knew that I
wanted it."

"You can get another one," Hannah replied.

"It was the only one there and it was an end-
of-the-season sale," Tatiana said, anguish clear
in her voice.

"Can't you share it?" Gregory asked.

They looked at their father as though he'd
grown antlers. "No!" they screamed.

Tatiana reached for the bag. "Tell her to give it
to me."

"I won't." Hannah moved it away. "I bought it fair and square."

"You're always ruining things for me."

"Let's see the skirt," Mariella said.

The two girls were stunned at first then moved closer and Hannah pulled the skirt out of a large overstuffed bag and held it up. It was an orange bias-cut silk A-line skirt, framed with ruffles around the hem.

"Oh, is that it?" she said, bored. "Let her keep it. It's not your color anyway and the cut is all wrong. Your younger sister only bought that to spite you."

Hannah's gaze sent daggers at Mariella.

Ignoring the seething teenager, Mariella rose from the couch and put her arm around Tatiana. She pulled her to the side.

"Now, it appears you're going to be going off to college soon," Mariella said pointing to the large sign that read Congratulations Graduate and a framed picture of Tatiana in her cap and gown. "And I'm sure you'll want to make a good impression. I suggest you get your hands on Moira Mason's *Fashion Guide for the College Girl* and start new. Moira is an associate of mine. Incidentally, her grandmother was Miss Jamaica in the '60s. Anyway, not everyone is born knowing how to dress. It's an art that few people study. But with practice it becomes effortless. If you have any questions, feel free to call me. I'll give your mother my direct number."

Tatiana smiled shyly. "I will." She turned to her younger sister. "And she's right, that skirt wouldn't have looked good on me anyway." She lowered her voice. "And it will look even worse on you." Tatiana left.

The younger sister sent them all an evil glare then flew up the stairs pounding her foot on each step.

Yolanda looked at Mariella surprised. "Well, I wouldn't have handled it that way, but it sure got results."

Mariella shrugged. "I grew up the eldest of four sisters. I became adept at putting out fires."

Ian grinned at her. "And perhaps starting some?"

"Perhaps," she said, grinning back.

As they drove home that evening, Ian said, "So you're the eldest?"

"Yes, I'm the eldest just like you."

"What makes you think I'm older than Josh?"

"You have that big brother air about you."

He thought for a moment then nodded, "Hmm, it would have been that way except for a couple of minutes."

She frowned. "Minutes?"

"Yes, he was born before I was."

"By minutes?"

"Yes." He sent her an odd glance. "Wait, you didn't know we were twins?"

"No."

"Hmm, I see. He doesn't like to talk about it much." He tapped his fingers on the steering wheel.

"My father took exactly ten pictures of him, but my face was plastered everywhere. It didn't seem fair."

"Is that why you hate your photograph being taken?"

"No, I told you." He winked at her. "I'm shy."

"You're a devil."

"Perhaps that, too." He was quiet then said, "My brother is brilliant, but my father never saw it because he didn't find him good-looking enough."

"I didn't think fathers worried about things like that," Mariella responded, taking out her compact to touch up her makeup.

"With Jeremiah he loved things of beauty."

"But he wasn't that much of a looker himself."

"Yes, that's just it. Being born 'plain' had caused him pain. He made up for his looks with the vast amount of wealth he accumulated. His looks didn't matter, he was a very rich man. But it also made him a target, and he didn't want that for his sons."

"So you made your father hate you so that he'd pay attention to Josh?"

He sent her a sly look. "I'm not that intellectually devious, but thanks for the compliment. No, it was simpler than that. I just didn't fit in." They were quiet the rest of the drive back to the hotel and Mariella was certain he wasn't going to say anything else when he dropped her off at the door, but he surprised her. "Did you enjoy the evening?" he asked.

"Yes."

"Good." He lightly touched her cheek. "And I wasn't kidding."

"About what?"

"I plan to make you Mariella Cooper." He briefly kissed her then turned. "Good night."

Mariella slowly closed the door, oddly impressed by his arrogance and pleased with yet another taste of those succulent lips. Perhaps it wasn't such a bad idea. She changed her mind the next day when he voted against one of her model selections. He and Donna chose a girl she thought completely wrong and wouldn't listen to her argument for one she felt would be perfect. Determined to give her selection a chance before the young lady left, Mariella met with her and scheduled a shoot on her own time.

"This probably isn't a good idea," Gen said as Mariella instructed the model, Teresa, for the shot.

"I don't care. It's my own time. They can't do anything to me."

"You do realize that her face is too round."

"Just wait until these pictures are developed, then you'll see how perfect she is. She has a nice fresh natural look—that's why I didn't want to use the lighting people."

"You couldn't afford them."

Mariella kept on shooting, pleased that the young woman needed minimal instruction.

Gen sighed. "That soft heart of yours is going to get you into a lot of trouble one day."

"This is a professional decision. This has nothing to do with my soft heart, which incidentally, I don't have."

Mariella instructed Teresa to remove the detachable skirt, revealing a pair of ravishing long legs. Mariella knew Gen didn't see what she did, but she was certain once the photos were developed she would.

The remainder of the day went as planned. Donna showed up at the shoot, Mariella wasn't sure why and didn't care to ask. She ignored her and by the end of the day felt completely satisfied with the pictures she had taken.

Later that evening, Mariella stopped by a rental studio, which Gen had contacted earlier to develop some of her photos. The owner, Campbell Watkins, was more than happy to oblige her, having seen Mariella's photos when she was with Desire. She agreed to take a picture with him that he would later blow up and frame. After using his darkroom, Mariella left that evening pleased with her work and nearly crashed into Ian as she exited the studio.

"What are you up to?" he said.

"What do you mean?"

"I mean the photos you took of Teresa."

She didn't care to ask how he'd found out. "I took her photos on my own time."

"Let me see them."

"I did both film and digital." She handed him the black-and-white photos she had developed.

Ian looked through them then took out his checkbook. "How much did you pay her?" When she told him, he gave a low whistle. "Tell me next time."

"So you'll use them?" she asked with growing excitement.

"No."

Her heart fell. "What?"

"They're good, but Jeremiah would not have used her. You and I know that. This is about him. Not you. You can keep these pictures for your own personal collection and try to stay focused."

"He has a point," Gen said as they sat in a late-night restaurant. "This is about Jeremiah's vision, not yours."

"Jeremiah would have listened a little. Not

much, but a little." She sighed. "I guess I just feel that everything is out of my hands. And I don't like being out of control. Like I'm just a hired hand."

"But it's going perfectly. We're on schedule. We'll be in Vermont soon and then the project will be over and soon you'll have your name associated with *Flash* magazine and doors will open wide."

"Yes, I guess you're right. So how is Josh?"

Her gaze fell. "He's fine."

"I've noticed you haven't been available for dinner recently."

Gen sipped her drink.

"Or lunch."

She continued to sip.

"And sometimes even breakfast."

She colored.

Mariella shrugged. "As long as you're enjoying yourself."

"I am."

"Have you told him yet?"

"No. Mariella, please don't bring that up. It's hard as it is."

"I'm sorry."

A woman passed by their table, then stopped and stared at Mariella. "I know you."

"Really?" Mariella said, used to such statements.

"Yes. You're the bitch who killed my daughter."

Chapter 11

Mariella's skin turned to ice. "I don't know what you're talking about."

"My daughter was fine until she wanted to be like you. Glamorous. Beautiful. Thin. She starved herself to death. How does it feel to sell little girls lies? Huh? You're a disgrace. You sleep around with old men and take drugs. Don't you care about those that look up to you? Of course not. You don't care about anyone. You're scum and should rot in hell." She grabbed a glass of water and threw it in Mariella's face.

Mariella wiped her face with a napkin, then slapped the woman so hard the woman went reeling back and crashed into a table. Mariella stood. "I suggest you get on some sort of medication to help you with your delusions."

"You evil bitch!"

Mariella went toward the woman, who was now sprawled on the ground but Gen grabbed her arm. Although still seething with anger, Mariella held her head high and left. The two drove back to the hotel in silence. But chaos broke loose when Ian read the paper the next day. He called Mariella to his hotel suite where he and Josh were waiting.

"What the hell is this?" he demanded, waving the paper, fury tingeing his words.

Mariella sat looking demure in an overstuffed Chippendale chair, swinging her foot determined to stay distant and cool. "Nothing."

Josh's gaze darted between them.

Ian read the headline. "Ex-Desire Model 'Mad Mariella' Attacks Fan." He tossed the paper down in disgust. "You consider that nothing?"

"It was a misunderstanding."

"What happened?"

"Nothing that needs to be repeated. Don't worry, this will all die down."

"This doesn't put *Flash* magazine in a good light. We can't be known for working with photographers who attack people."

"It wasn't my fault. She—"

"I don't care what she did. It's your behavior

that's the problem. You cannot act this way. I know you're used to having your diva behavior splashed around in New York but when you work for me you'd better learn how to control yourself. If I see an incident like this again…"

"You'll fire me?" she finished.

"No," he said with a cold grin. "I don't want to reward you for bad behavior. Don't worry, I'll think of something."

She jumped to her feet. "If you'd just listen."

"I'm through listening."

"You don't understand." Mariella began to walk over to a large window. Ian startled her by grabbing her arm and turning her around.

"Really? You think I don't understand what it's like to be attacked. Look, I've been spat at, called names, had my life threatened and worse, but my name was never found in the gossip columns because I know how to handle myself. I did my job and that was it. Learn to control your temper." He waved a dismissive hand. "You're free to go. I have to get this mess cleared up. Unless you have some great ideas you'd like to share."

She glared at him then her eyes turned cool. "All right," she said simply and calmly walked out.

Ian stared at the closed door, his anger turning into worry. That exit wasn't like her.

But Josh was thrilled. "Man, you really threw

it at her. For a moment she looked mad enough to hammer nails into the wall with her fist."

"But that's not how she left," Ian said quietly.

Josh didn't hear him. "She's irresponsible, irrational and dangerous. Do you think the woman will sue?"

Ian continued to stare at the door. "Probably."

"But you showed her who's boss. That's the Ian I know. He won't let some hotheaded diva get the better of him."

Ian didn't hear his brother's words of praise or feel the weight of his victory. He had won. He'd defeated, demeaned, chastised and criticized her. He'd also made her leave without her dignity. He was used to being ruthless, but this time he'd gone too far. He'd hurt her.

He wasn't known for being a kind or considerate person and his arrogant pride was part of his reputation. But today he felt like a true SOB. He hadn't listened when she'd offered to explain. He hadn't softened when his words had forced her to cringe. He'd gone in for the kill as though she were one of the other models he'd grown up despising. She'd been the target of his venom and he regretted every moment.

He'd been fooled by her cool demeanor, by her chilly tone and appearance of nonchalance, but when he'd cracked through the veneer instead of treading carefully he'd rammed through. She'd never let him close now and he wouldn't blame her. The Atlanta trip had been a complete disaster for him. He always seemed to say or do the wrong thing. He'd have to find a way to fix that.

He spun around and pulled out his laptop. "Get Angus on the phone."

"Our attorney's name is Anthony."

"Just get him on the phone," Ian snapped.

"What are you going to do with Mariella?"

"I'm going to take care of her," he said, not caring how his brother would misinterpret his words.

Mariella didn't slam the door when she returned to her hotel room. She didn't throw her purse on the couch or toss her keys on the table. She went to the window and stared out thinking of how much she hated Ian Cooper. What she hated more was that she'd actually thought she could explain things to him when she never explained herself to anyone. He was the most heartless barbarian she'd ever met and she couldn't wait until the project ended and she never had to set eyes on him again. But she could be as cold as he was and she would be.

The phone rang, jarring her out of her thoughts. She ignored it and it quieted. A few minutes later it rang again. She reluctantly picked it up.

"Hello?"

"Mariella," her sister Isabella said, her voice full of sympathy. "I saw the paper. I'm so sorry."

Mariella fell into a couch; a well of pain gripped her heart and filled her eyes with tears. Suddenly she wanted to be home: Home with her sisters. Home away from all the ugliness of this business. Home to people who knew and loved her.

"You know how reporters are," she said, trying to sound flippant.

"You deserve better. I read that story and couldn't believe it. I knew that wasn't you. What happened?"

The tears fell. Here was someone who would be on her side, who cared about her version of the story. She told Isabella everything and her sister was appropriately outraged. "And Ian has been horrible to me. He chastised me and even threatened me."

"What? He said he'd fire you?"

"Worse."

"What could be worse?"

"He'd think of something. He acted as though this incident was all my fault. As though my behavior was out of line. Isabella, that woman threw a drink in my face. I think she was trying to disfigure me. You would have done the same, right?" When Isabella didn't respond, Mariella said, "Right?"

"There are always different ways to handle a situation."

"Are you saying that he was right?" Mariella said, offended.

"No, it's just that…well…because you're such a recognizable person you have to handle yourself differently. Remember when Mom scolded you for putting salt in the lemonade of Aunt Lynette because you wanted to get back at her for letting cousin Grace use your favorite hair slides?"

"Yes."

"She said that a lady always handles herself as though the other person is behaving disgracefully."

"I was never a perfect lady, Izzy."

Her sister laughed. "None of us were."

Mariella shook her head. "It just would have been nice if he'd listened…." The memory of his words pierced her again and renewed the anger she felt. She'd tried to open up to him and he'd turned her away. She soon steeled herself from the emotions. "But I don't care what he thinks. I can't wait until this project is over."

"Do you want me to come down there for a few days?"

"No, we're leaving here soon, but thanks for the offer."

"Okay. Love you."

"Love you too." She gripped the phone. "Izzy?"

"Yes?"

She loosened her grip. "Nothing. Bye." Mariella hung up the phone and drew her knees to her chest, for a moment wishing she were a little child in the safety of her father's arms. But she soon let the feelings pass and let her feet fall to the floor. She was a grown woman and both her parents were dead.

Mariella looked at her schedule for the afternoon and was about to go soak in a bath when someone knocked on the door. She answered and saw Ian. He looked at her as though their last conversation hadn't happened. "Have your bags packed within an hour," he said.

She rested her hip against the door frame. "So you've decided to fire me after all. Do you want to quickly ship me off to New York?"

"No, we're going to Vermont."

She straightened, suspicious. "But the shoot's not finished. Where's Gen?"

"We have enough for the Atlanta layout." He glanced at his watch. "Meet me in the lobby in an hour." He turned and left.

Although she wanted to argue with him about the way he commanded her, she was thrilled at the prospect of leaving Georgia, getting the Vermont shoot completed early and putting Ian out of her life for good. She quickly packed her clothes, although she was careful to make sure to pack them well. She left money for the housekeeping service and a note for Gen, to add her share, and answered the three surveys left on her desk. She was on her third one when someone pounded on her door again.

"I'll be there in a minute," she said.

The pounding continued. She swore and opened the door. "Don't you know how to knock?"

Ian frowned. "What's wrong?"

"Nothing. I said I'd be there in a minute."

"And I said to meet me downstairs in an hour," he said through clenched teeth. He held up his watch for her to see. "It is now an hour *and* fifteen minutes."

"I'm almost done." Mariella turned and went back to her desk. "I was never a fast writer."

Ian paused then said in a too-quiet tone, "What are you writing?"

"My comments on the service." She finished her last survey then placed it in the provided envelope.

He closed the door behind him. "Why?"

"Because I feel it is my duty to give my honest opinion. How can people improve if they don't know where they are lacking? I also left money for the housekeeping of course and then had to attend to—"

Ian moved around then glanced at a suitcase on her bed, his manner quick and impatient. "I don't care. Are you packed?"

"Of course."

He grabbed her suitcases. "Then let's go."

Mariella followed Ian outside to the front where his car was parked. She watched him put her suitcases in the trunk and close it.

"Where is everyone else?" she asked.

"They're staying."

"But I thought you said *we* were leaving."

"We are." He opened the door. "Get in."

"I thought you meant the team."

"No, I meant us," he said in clipped tones. "We're going to Vermont before everyone else. Now get in."

Mariella opened her mouth but the expression on Ian's face stopped her. She sighed and got in the car.

Chapter 12

The flight to Vermont was uneventful after which Ian and Mariella took a small commuter plane to reach their final destination. Mariella gasped at the aerial view of Vermont's highest mountain, Mount Mansfield, and the ending of Vermont's famous fall season. Thankfully, Ian proved to be a quiet companion. She had no desire to speak to him. Once they touched down in the small airport, they took a taxi to a local car rental.

"You should have chosen somewhere closer to the city," Mariella said as they walked toward a medium-size car he'd rented. It wasn't as glamorous as the one Ian had rented in Atlanta, but at least it was spacious.

"You'll like the location once we reach it," he said.

After an hour, Mariella wondered if they ever would. Finally, Ian turned off a main road onto a little dirt road. Tall evergreen trees lined either side. There were no streetlights. Mariella was glad to see they would soon reach their destination. Over the radio, they had heard reports of a major change in the weather. The sky soon darkened from gathering storm clouds. Suddenly, the clouds opened up, drenching the car in heavy sheets of rain.

The downpour turned the dirt road into a muddy river and the car tires fought to grip the ground—sometimes succeeding and sometimes not—forcing the car to go up and down like a boat in the middle of an ocean. Although Ian had driven through different types of terrain all over the world, the rental car was no match for the elements and abruptly halted.

"Why are you stopping?" Mariella asked.

Ian looked at her in disbelief. "What do you mean, 'Why am I stopping?'"

"It's a simple question. Don't be upset if you don't know the answer."

"The car is stuck. Or haven't you noticed the wheels turning?"

"Fine." She unlatched her seat belt. "Get out then."

"What?" His voice cracked.

"You're going to push it, aren't you? I'll steer."

"I'm not pushing anything in this weather."

"Then what are you going to do?"

"I'm going to wait."

"For what?"

"For the rain to stop."

She threw up her hands. "But that could be hours."

"If you feel like pushing, that's fine with me." He flashed a wicked grin. "I'll steer."

She glared at him then folded her arms. After a few moments she said, "Why did you choose this place?"

"I told you why."

"Someone could die out here and no one would know."

"That's a tempting thought," he grumbled.

"What?"

"Nothing."

She shot him a glance. "What happened in Georgia wasn't my fault."

"Of course," he said, sarcastic. "You're completely blameless. Nothing that happens is your fault. Those pictures of you in my father's bedroom aren't your fault, the papers calling you

'Mad Mariella' or 'Deranged Duvall,' aren't your fault. You're just a victim of life."

"I know I'm not perfect. But at least I'm not too arrogant to admit when I'm wrong."

"What do you mean?"

"You're lost and you made a mistake by having us come here."

"No, I didn't."

"If I had been in charge of this journey we wouldn't be stuck on a muddy road in the middle of nowhere."

Ian sighed, trying to keep his patience. "We're not in the middle of nowhere. I know where we are."

"How far is the house?"

He gestured to the darkness in front of them. "Straight ahead. I'm sure it's not far. Probably just a couple miles up the road. Look, I didn't expect it to rain this hard."

"You could have rented a car with front-wheel drive."

"Oh well." He lowered the back of his seat.

She watched him, confused. "What are you doing?"

"I'm going to sleep." He leaned his head back and closed his eyes. "Wake me up when the weather clears."

Mariella sat quietly a moment then said, "I'm cold."

Ian kept his eyes closed. "Then get clothes from the trunk."

She stared out the window in dismay. "But it's raining."

"Then see if the back seats pull down."

She turned to him, surprised at such a clever suggestion, then climbed into the back seat. She pulled down the seat and managed to grab her bag. She pulled out a sweater and put it on. "I'm hungry too."

"Hmm."

With such an unhelpful response Mariella decided to busy herself with the suitcase. Ian tried to sleep, but kept hearing Mariella zipping and unzipping things. Then he heard her gasp. "I don't believe it!"

Ian sat up and turned. "What?"

"Everything you own is black." She lifted one of his briefs. "Except for these, they're gray."

"What are you doing in my suitcase?"

"I am bored," she said, rummaging through the rest of his clothes. "What else do you expect me to do?"

"I don't care. Close it up."

She lifted out a cashmere sweater. "Hmm, this looks warm. I'll wear this instead."

His tone hardened. "Mariella."

"Don't worry, I'll be very gentle with it. Ooh, it feels wonderful." She pulled it on. "Ah, much better."

"Now close my suitcase."

"May I make a suggestion?"

"No."

"You would look great in maroon. You'd look great in any color, but since you prefer dark colors I think it would be a nice start."

"Close it. Now."

"Or perhaps navy blue. Yes, that's better. A nice navy blue would suit you. It can look like black in certain lights. I would try it."

"Mariella," he said in warning.

"You're not listening to me."

"No."

She sighed, resigned. "Fine. Let me just fold everything back."

"You don't need to fold anything."

"But I messed them up when I took out the sweater."

"I don't care."

"You had everything so neat and orderly. All right, I'll close it," she said quickly when he began to rise from his reclined position. She stopped when she saw something metallic. "Wait, what's this?" She reached in and pulled out a granola bar. She glared at him. "I thought you said you didn't have any food."

"I didn't say that."

"But I said I was hungry and you didn't offer me anything."

"I would have if I really thought you were hungry."

"But I am."

"No, you're just bored."

"What else do you have hidden in here?"

He scrambled into the back seat. "None of your business."

His statement came too late. Mariella had pushed aside his other clothes and uncovered his food stash. She folded her arms and stared at him. "Did you plan this on purpose?"

He furrowed his brow, confused. "Plan what?"

"Getting us stuck."

He looked at her for a long moment then said in a dry tone, "Of course. That was the plan all along. I wanted to get us stuck here on a dark muddy road in a place where we may freeze to death just so that I could spend time alone with you."

She frowned. "You don't need to be sarcastic."

"Then don't ask silly questions."

She gestured to the case. "Then what's all this? Do you usually carry this much food with you?"

"Yes."

"Why?"

"Let's just say that I have an unhappy memory of being lost in Gambia with no food or drink and don't want to repeat the experience."

"I see. What were you doing there?"

"Taking pictures."

"Of what?"

"Things."

"What things?"

He shrugged.

"I'm trying to have a conversation with you or is having a conversation as difficult for you as having good manners?"

He smiled.

"Fine." She reached for another bar. "I might as well eat something."

He snatched it from her and tossed it back in the case. "You only need one."

"Well, I want two."

He zipped up the case. "You're having one. Enjoy it."

"Is being a bastard a studied practice or a defect at birth?"

Ian took the remaining bar from her hand.

She reached for it. "Give that back."

He blocked her by turning to the side then pulled down the wrapper. "Why?"

"Because it's mine."

"So what?" He took a bite. "I'm a bastard, remember?"

"Every minute." She looked out the window. "If I knew the house was close by I'd walk there right now just to get away from you."

"I have an umbrella."

She continued to stare out the window. She felt restless and annoyed. Everything about this project seemed to be a disaster. She felt something fall into her lap and glanced down and saw a granola bar.

"I'm not hungry," she said, looking up at him.

"Then save it for later." His eyes met hers. "I'm sorry about Georgia."

She narrowed her eyes. "Don't start being nice to me. My hatred for you keeps me warm."

He stretched his arm out the length of the seat. "There's another way to stay warm."

She widened her eyes. "You're unbelievable."

He bowed his head. "Thank you."

"It wasn't a compliment."

He shrugged. "I think it is."

She shook her head in amazement. "How can you think about sex at a time like this?"

He raised his brows. "What else am I supposed to think about? I've already eaten something."

"And that's the stretch of your imagination. Food and sex?"

"No."

"What else?"

"I'm glad we didn't drink too much. Seeing all this rain would be a nightmare."

She raised her gaze to the ceiling. "I'm sorry I asked."

"I'm just being practical, Your Highness. Now come over here."

She jerked her head back. "I'm not sleeping with you in order to keep warm."

"I wasn't asking you to. I have a blanket," Ian said, pulling it from his case. "But it won't stretch over there."

"My goodness, do you have a tent in there as well?"

"You'll find out later. Now come on."

"I'm fine where I am."

"You stubborn…" He took a deep breath. "Fine, you win."

"What are you doing?" she demanded when he began to stand.

"If the mountain won't move, I must bring myself to the mountain." He settled down beside her and covered them both with the blanket. "Feel free to wrap your arms around me."

"I'd rather hug a cactus."

"I'm much softer." He put her arm around his chest.

She yanked it away.

He put it back. "Stop being stubborn. I know that you're freezing…and stop trying to squeeze me. It doesn't hurt and I'm very ticklish."

She released her grip then grumbled. "You're enjoying this."

"Yes, very much." He paused. "Probably a little too much, but you'll help me deal with that later."

She knew what he meant and felt it too

although she tried to keep still. She tried not to think of all that could happen under the blanket. What if his hand wandered over to her leg, or her thigh or even higher? She shifted, her thigh brushing his and sending a sensation that felt like a lightning bolt through her, making her jump.

"I'm not going to do anything," he said.

More's the pity. "I know." She grabbed her granola bar, feeling foolish. Being with a man shouldn't affect her this much. She'd been with several. Too bad this one smelled so good and felt so good and could probably turn this blanket into an electrical one with just a glance. She stole glances at his profile, trying to catch glimpses of the man underneath but failing. Like her he knew how to control his features to reveal only what he wanted to.

"Do you sometimes miss your old life?" she asked, desperate to speak so that her mind wouldn't wander.

"Yes."

"Do you hate your father for making you have to leave it?"

"No. He didn't make me leave it. My heart had left it years before I stopped."

"Why?"

"I was a different person." Before she could ask him what he meant by that he said, "What did that woman say to you at the restaurant?"

"It doesn't matter. Why?"

"Because I'm curious."

"She said I killed her daughter, but why should you care?"

"I do care. Tremendously," he said with quiet emphasis. "I just didn't want to. Not that much. I'm sorry." He took a deep breath. "You can't let them get to you. I've tried to live my entire life without feeling. I've trained myself to be an observer, distant, objective. But when I saw your face that morning—you were cool as usual, but then you wanted to explain and I couldn't let you. I couldn't let you reveal yourself to me as though it was too much of a responsibility and I'd have to reveal myself to you. I couldn't risk that, especially not in front of Josh. I wanted you to protect yourself. I handled it all wrong and I'm truly sorry." He smiled ruefully. "And I can tell by the look on your face that you don't believe a word I've said."

"A woman has to be very careful who she chooses to trust."

"Men have the same problem."

She searched his face. "It's just that you guard your emotions so well."

"And you don't?"

"I don't know if this is real or another game."

"What's between us is real." He kissed her, leaving no doubt of his desire for her. The full emotion of his kiss left her stunned for this was not a kiss of lust. The real Ian Cooper held her in his arms. There was no bid of dominance or surrender. They met as equals. Equals in wanting, in needing, in desire. Soon their passion was too much for the back seat to hold.

Ian pulled back and swore. "You're right. This is a stupid car."

"Probably for the best."

"Maybe," he said, slipping a hand under her sweater.

"Ow! Your hands are freezing."

He drew back and rubbed his hands together. "Sorry."

"I can warm them up faster." She took his hands and placed them between her thighs, then squeezed them together. "Better?"

His eyes clung to hers. "No." He reached for the front of her jeans.

"What are you doing?" she demanded when he drew down the zipper.

"Keeping my hands warm." He pulled down her jeans then stroked the inside of her leg. "That's better." His voice deepened into huskiness. "Man, I want you."

"You have me." But even as she said the words she knew it wasn't enough. Her body ached to be closer to him, to become one. "My hands are a little chilly too," she said, slipping them under his shirt, the muscles of his chest constricted at her touch and she could feel the racing of his heart.

"Then I'd better warm you up." He removed her panties.

She looked at him in surprise. "I thought we weren't going to..."

"We're not," he said then slipped his fingers inside her, stirring up a spiral of ecstasy until she climaxed. He grinned with masculine pride from the joy on her face.

"Next time that will be me," he promised.

"I thought it was you."

"Let's just say you'll be getting more."

She reached over and rested her hand on the hard bulge pressing against the front of his trousers. "Perhaps I should see what I'll be getting."

He gently seized her wrist and placed her hand back in her lap. "Honey, if you touch me like that, things could get out of hand. You'll just have to imagine."

She cocked her head to the side and raised a challenging brow. "I have a big imagination."

"Then you won't be disappointed."

She shook her head in amazement. "Your humility is breathtaking."

He bowed. "Thank you," he said then stroked her thigh. "Wait, what's this?"

He moved the blanket and looked down at a light slightly raised scar.

"Oh that, I usually put makeup on it. A tiger gave it to me."

"A tiger?"

She told him about the incident and then about another in Florida where a jellyfish stung her and her foot swelled. She was about to tell him about a harrowing incident in Italy, but stopped when she noticed he was getting upset although he was trying to listen without judgment. "But I'm all right now," she said quickly.

He gave a terse nod.

She wiggled back into her panties and jeans. "Thanks for listening."

He nodded again.

She wrapped her arms around him and rested her head against his chest and after a few moments felt him relax. He held her snugly and she felt all fear dissipate. She could trust him. "Sometimes I do think about that woman." She gripped his shirt, her voice low and tight. "When she accused me of killing her daughter for a second I thought she was right. I thought that I'd killed her. That I'd made her so unhappy that she didn't want to live anymore and I wanted to die."

"Don't say that."

"It feels good to say it because it's true. There are moments when you have to face hard truths. I'm glad I'm doing something new and I'm going to succeed at it."

"Yes." He pressed her head to his chest and wrapped the blanket tighter around them. "Now go to sleep."

She did. He watched morning come in its bright glory. Slowly touching the leaves and the mountains in the distance then stared straight ahead and swore. He didn't know much, but he knew one thing. When Mariella woke up, she was going to kill him.

Chapter 13

He felt her awaken and said, "Don't get angry."

"Why would I be angry?"

He nodded to the windshield. She looked and stared then burst into laughter.

He sent her an odd look. "You think this is funny?"

"Yes, I love to see what you consider a couple of *miles* up the road."

The house stood only a few yards away. It was a massive stately mansion, covered in vine with two large columns at the entrance. On the roof you could see at least four chimneys while grandiose windows looked down on them. The shrubbery and plants lining the house reflected hours and hours of meticulous gardening.

"I'm glad you're taking this so well," Ian said.

She grinned. "You mean you're lucky."

He nodded. "Yes, that too."

Mariella stepped out into the mud. It covered up to her ankles. She swore as she trudged through, then noticed a fox in the distance. It darted between the trees. "Oh look." She pointed. "It's beautiful."

"It seems to be following us."

"And having an easier time," she said lifting her shoe out of the mud, making a sucking noise as she raised it.

They made their way to the front entrance. Then they saw a smaller residence to the side of the house in the distance. With no reply to their knocking at the house, Ian decided to see if anyone was in the cottage. No one answered. Ian walked back to the main house.

"You do realize that it's freezing?" Mariella asked, somehow managing not to let her teeth chatter.

"At least put your suitcase down."

"I'm not resting anything down in this mud."

"Wait a minute." Ian disappeared around the back of the house and came back holding a key.

"Don't worry, I made arrangements with the owner that if no one was home, he told me where to find the key." Ian opened the door then reached for the light switch. Nothing happened.

"It seems the power is out. Mariella, you stay here, I'll get the rest of our things."

Mariella started looking around. She was cold and miserable and was not in the mood to spend a day or worse yet another night freezing. Once Ian had finished bringing in all the luggage and photography equipment, he and Mariella went looking for anything to keep them warm.

In the kitchen, they found a note telling them where to find a kerosene heater and the fuel and also where canned food was stored, plus batteries, etc.

"They must regularly lose power," Ian said.

Mariella rolled her eyes. "That's a cheery thought." In the pantry, they noticed a battery-powered radio and took it back with them to the main living room, to listen and find out what was going on with the weather. The news wasn't good. Due to the unexpected storm, no flights would be going in or out of the airport. In addition, the announcer stated that there would be an early winter snowstorm coming later that night that would likely turn all the rain into dangerous ice.

"Where are you going?" Mariella asked when Ian headed toward the stairs.

"I'm going to call Josh. I'll see if I can get a signal."

"What am I supposed to do?"

"Make yourself useful."

"Doing what?"

"I don't know, start a fire or something." He disappeared upstairs and managed to call his brother before the battery ran out on his cell phone.

"How are things?" Josh asked.

"Oh, it's great. We spent the night in the car and now we are in a cold empty house and another storm might hit."

"We'll see when we can come in, but you might have to wait a week."

"A week? Are you kidding?"

"No, they say when that area is corded off it takes time to clear the roads. Nothing is going to happen until everything is deemed safe. I'm sorry."

"Me too."

"I'm going to have nightmares of you alone with that woman."

"I'll be fine."

"With *Mariella?*"

"Yes."

"Duvall?"

"Yes," he said, impatiently. "I'd better go and see how she's doing." He hung up then went into the living room where a roaring fire greeted him. He halted and stared amazed. "What is that?"

Mariella frowned. "What does it look like?"

"But how did it get there?"

"I made it. You told me to start a fire."

"I know but—"

She folded her arms and sent him a smug look. "You didn't think I could."

"No, I didn't think you *would.*"

"You don't grow up in upstate New York and not know how to survive the winters there. And I'd never sit in a cold room just to spite you."

He knelt in front of the fire and warmed his hands. "Good job."

"Thanks. So what is the status?"

"It seems that we may be stuck here a couple of days."

"Days?"

"Yes. So I guess we should settle in."

They spent the rest of the day adjusting to their situation. The first place Ian raided was the kitchen and to his delight the refrigerator was stocked with prepared dishes including a potato salad, bacon/turkey sandwiches, and a fifteen-bean soup. Not wanting to bother heating up the soup, they decided on the salad and sandwiches.

Once they finished eating they agreed to stay in what appeared to be the family room. It was a smaller room than the formal living room and could be heated up quickly with the kerosene heater. Ian was careful to make sure it was positioned away from anything. The room was very comfortable with insulated curtains, thick carpeting and two sleep sofas. It appeared that the family was either large, or used to entertaining a number of guests. Mariella quickly selected the sofa close to the heater. She also found a divider that she borrowed from the living room, to provide some privacy and a place for her to hang up her clothing. She began pulling out the other bed.

"We're not going to need two beds," Ian said.

"I always keep my options open."

"Well, I'm only giving you one."

Mariella completed making the second bed knowing it best not to reply. Within several minutes the kerosene lamp heated the room. That evening, with the radio playing in the background, they had dinner. This time they had soup with several glasses of red wine, which had also been left for them. Ian had found a cast iron pot, which he used on the fireplace in the living room.

Once dinner was over Mariella sat on her bed and stared at the heater, bored. "What happens next?"

Ian lay back on his sofa bed. "Well, in five minutes I'm going to make love to you, you're going to enjoy it, then I'll go to bed." He raised a mischievous brow. "You can decide what to do with yourself after that."

Chapter 14

"Why five minutes?" Mariella asked, intrigued.

"Planning."

"Oh?"

"Yes, I'm considering my options: the sofa, bed or floor."

"That covers one minute."

"I'll have to wrap my friend."

Mariella walked over and straddled him. "And then?"

"My approach."

She unbuttoned his shirt. "And then?"

"I haven't thought much further."

"Good." She kissed his throat.

"Now I remember."

She stopped and looked at him.

"Nope, I've lost it again."

"You can put your arms around me."

"Not yet."

She stared at him in disbelief. "You're really going to make me wait?"

"I'm making *us* wait."

"I might change my mind."

"I'll change it back for you."

She moved away. "I don't think you can." She slid off the bed and returned to hers.

He clasped his hands behind his head and watched her. "Good. I love a challenge."

She turned her back to him and picked up a magazine from her suitcase. However, she couldn't focus on it. She kept waiting for the puma to pounce. The three minutes that lapsed felt like years. Anticipation heightening with every passing second until she thought she couldn't stand it. Then the three minutes were over. He didn't move.

She wouldn't tell him that the minutes had passed. She wouldn't admit how he'd made her ache for his touch, how he'd left her wanting and waiting. Right now she could take a fire poker and stab him with it.

"Ready?" he asked, his voice warm against her ear.

She jumped. "Don't do that."

"I thought you'd like the element of surprise." He drew her close and kissed away any protest. She didn't offer him any. "Don't be nervous."

"I'm not."

"Then why are you trembling?"

"Don't confuse irritation for passion."

"Why not?" he growled; then he nipped the tip of her ear with his teeth. "You enjoy being irritated with me." He took down one bra strap. "I'm not making love to the ex-Desire model." He removed the other strap. "Or the photographer." He unlatched it. "I'm making love to a woman who is unmatched in courage." He pressed his lips to her bare shoulder. "In talent." He kissed the other shoulder. "And intelligence." He kissed her mouth.

When he pulled away she said, "You forgot to say 'in beauty.'"

"No, I didn't."

"Will you ever tell me I'm beautiful?"

"Does the sun need to be told that it's hot?"

"But—"

He kissed her, but an uneasiness lingered inside her. He didn't understand how men's words of admiration thrilled her, aroused her and gave her power. But when he looked at her tenderly as though she were an ordinary woman—no, *his woman*—it made her feel vulnerable and possessed. That was exactly what he was doing when he soothed the ache between her legs by entering her. He claimed her as his own with every touch and caress. What scared her most was that she didn't mind. She surrendered to it, then made a claim of her own until their lovemaking became primitive, hot and wild. When they were done, they collapsed, exhausted by their own raw emotions.

Ian rose early the next morning and went outside. He needed the crisp cold air to temper the mixture of emotions warring inside him. The storm had brought four inches of snow, blanketing the scene in white and it was beautiful. It had been a long time before he'd been able to see beauty like this and he could even admit that he was happy. Life was good. Almost perfect. He went to the pile of firewood at the side of the house, whistling. He stopped when he saw a spot of red marring the white surface. He followed the spots and found the mangled body of a fox.

He stumbled back as though he'd been punched in the gut. All his joy vanished. Even in this seemingly peaceful place reality's cruel grasp had reached him.

"What are you doing out here?" Mariella said, coming up to him.

He spun around. "Go back inside."

"I was only…what's wrong?"

"Nothing. I told you to go inside."

"But if something's wrong—" She stopped and saw it. "Oh no."

"Go inside."

She touched his sleeve. "It's okay. You don't have to protect me." She took his hand. "Come on, let's go have some breakfast."

He didn't eat. The sight of the dead fox haunted him like the year after he'd taken pictures of children and one of them disappeared. They'd found his body years later. The carefree photographer of those photos had disappeared too and he'd buried him. That afternoon Ian went back to see the dead fox, he had to face it, but it was gone. There was no blood. Nothing. As though it had never been there. He rushed back inside. "Where is it?"

Mariella looked up from her makeup case where she'd been playing with different lipstick colors. "Where is what?"

"The fox."

"What fox?"

"The dead fox that was there this morning."

She lifted her compact and powdered her nose. "I didn't see a dead fox this morning."

"Yes, you did. We saw it together."

She snapped the compact closed. "Saw what together?"

Ian opened his mouth then closed it catching on to her ploy. "Forget it."

She sent him a significant look. "Yes, I think that's a good idea."

But he couldn't. He tried to shut off his mind. Things die every day. He was stupid to believe the universe was punishing him for his moment of happiness. They spent the rest of the day exploring the house and then each other. They found books and read passages and discussed them—they made each other laugh and shared private thoughts. Ian pushed the fox from his mind, but that night he tossed and turned. He couldn't allow himself to enjoy the warm body next to him and revel in her beauty. He'd never tell her how much her beauty affected him, she already held enough power over him.

How could he lie beside her taking pleasure in her softness, listening to the silence around him when people were dying and starving? Cathleen always liked to remind him of that. How he'd grown up privileged while others were suffering. He'd been determined to make a difference. But how was he making a difference now? He felt useless and yet that was the man Mariella admired. If he'd been the Ian of before, the cynical photojournalist—the Ian he somehow still was—would they still be together?

As he struggled with his thoughts, Mariella struggled with hers. She could sense his unease, but couldn't understand it. The death of the beau-

tiful fox saddened her but hadn't affected her as
it did him. She rested her chin on his bare chest.

"Can't sleep?" she asked.

"No."

"Want to tell me about it?"

He shook his head then said, "Why did you
love my father?"

"Why did you hate him?"

"I didn't. We just didn't always get along."

"I loved him as a friend."

"And you were willing to do anything for him?"

"What do you mean?"

"Why did you let everyone believe that the
drugs were yours?"

She sat up startled. "How did you...?" She
pulled the covers close. "They were mine."

"But you got them for him, didn't you?"

She was quiet then lowered her gaze. "He
was dying and I felt helpless. I wanted to do
whatever he wanted to somehow ease his suffering. I didn't see any harm in it." She met his
gaze. "No one understood our relationship. He
said that the herbs would help him, I wanted to
help him the way I hadn't been able to help..."
She took a deep breath. "My parents." She
touched his face in a light, fleeting gesture. "I
know about ugliness, I know about death and
disease. I know about despair and destitution. I
know humiliation."

"Those photographs of the children were taken when I was eighteen."

"You were very talented then."

"Yes, and I knew it. From that age to about twenty-three I had an overinflated ego. I knew I was good-looking, talented and rich. You wouldn't have liked me very much then."

"Who says I like you now?"

He smiled, sliding his hand to the curve of her hip. "I think you're warming to me."

"So what changed you?"

"Two things. One of those kids was murdered."

"I'm sorry. And two?"

"I met…I met my wife. She wasn't from my world and wasn't impressed with my pictures. She told me everything that was wrong. I fell in love with her instantly. She wasn't worried about her weight or her looks, she was passionate about her work. I learned from her. We traveled all over the world. Then in Gambia. I felt uneasy. I wasn't sure about the driver, but she went along with everything. We were ambushed. They just shot her. While I was standing there. She was dead before she hit the ground. In the movies you see the wounded linger. I still dream about having a moment with her, having the chance to cradle her in my arms, but that wasn't how it happened.

"I don't remember leaving the country or arriving back home. About a year of my life is blank to me; but after that I couldn't see joy. I envy your ability to see beauty and light."

She stared at him. "Claiming her darkness as your own won't keep her alive. Her memory is enough. You don't have to deny beauty or pain. It just is. You can't hurt enough to ease someone else's suffering, you can't weep enough to stop someone's pain. You can only do your best to help others and enjoy your life."

"I don't know if I can," he said, his voice hollow.

"Let me help you. I'm going to close my eyes and I want you to tell me what you see in this room."

"I see the remains of a cobweb and a shadow of a lamp on the wall, buckled hallway and couch that has been sat in too many times. Dark paneled walls and a fire. That's it."

"Okay, now you close your eyes."

"You think you'll see something different?"

"Just close your eyes."

He did.

"Okay, what do you see?"

"I see us."

He opened his eyes. "You can't see that."

"Yes, I can."

"How can you see us?"

She pointed. "That mirror. I always know when there is a mirror in a room. It's a gift."

"I didn't even notice it."

"I know. For an observer you miss a lot."

Over the next two days, they settled into a routine. Mariella had found some salmon and had cut it into thin strips and "cooked" it by pouring lemon juice on it. A skill she said she had learned from her father when she had gone on camping trips with him as a child. She also set aside a small jar of olive oil to use as a daily moisturizer, which she dutifully applied. Then there was the unforgettable moment when she applied mayonnaise to her hair as a deep conditioner and soaked her feet in a baking soda and vinegar mixture. They both experimented with dishes over the fire using the cast iron pot. Mariella's jambalaya went well, but Ian's attempt at macaroni and cheese did not. They found some old photo albums, several musical instruments and also played board games in the evening.

On the fifth day electricity returned. They celebrated by going for a walk. Mariella took her camera and snapped images of the landscape. Then she turned the camera on Ian.

He moved to the side, his tone accusatory. "What are you doing?"

She positioned her camera until he was in the frame again. "I'm going to take a picture."

"I don't like my picture being taken."

"Why not?" she challenged. "It's no big deal. I just want to take a picture of—" She stopped.

"Of what?"

The man I love. She finished the sentence silently but the impact of it nearly made her legs collapse beneath her. She gripped the camera, afraid her trembling fingers might make her drop it. She was wrong, it was just a passing notion. She didn't love him. She couldn't love him. She refused to. No matter how his eyes, which she'd once thought so cold and without feeling, could warm her heart. No matter how tenderly he held her in his arms or listened to her fears, she would not succumb to such a dangerous and foolish emotion.

Ian took a step toward her, concerned. "What's wrong?"

She took a step back and stiffened her spine. "Nothing. I was just thinking." She smiled tremulously. "I just had a horrible thought."

Ian folded his arms and feigned a pained look. "That's comforting. You look at me and then have a horrible thought. What was it about?"

She moved her shoulders in a dismissive gesture. "It was nothing really." She lifted her camera although her hands were still unsteady. "Now smile."

He moved out of her view. "No. I told you I don't like having my picture taken."

She lowered the camera, sighing with frustration and thankful that his stubborn side pushed away her foolish thoughts. "Come on. I just want to take a picture of a man in the woods on a snowy day."

"I still don't like it."

"Please."

"Okay." He turned his back to her. "How about this? I've been told I have a nice head shape."

She jumped in front of him. "I want to show your face."

He walked past her, over to a tree and placed his palm against the trunk, his head held down. In his dark clothes he was a striking contrast to the white snow around him.

"Ian, I just want you to see what I see."

He sent her a cautious look. "What will you do with the picture?"

"What do you mean?"

"Who will you show it to?"

She could see him weakening and controlled her growing excitement. "Nobody," she promised. "I'll keep it in my own private collection."

He chewed his lower lip. "Is that a promise?"

"Yes."

He straightened. "A solemn vow?"

"Yes."

He ambled toward her and looked deep in her eyes.

She pressed her lips against his. "There. Sealed with a kiss."

His voice deepened into huskiness. "There's another way to seal a bargain."

"Well, we're not doing that here. Now stop stalling. I'm going to take your picture."

"All right," he said without enthusiasm. "Just don't tell me what to do."

"I won't." Of course she couldn't help herself. Once Mariella was behind the camera, the photographer in her took hold and she told him how to hold his head, and angled him in certain poses. At first he balked, but she made him relax and eventually got him to smile. When she was done she handed the camera to him. "Now it's your turn."

He looked at it as though it were a foreign object. "To do what?"

"To take pictures."

He looked around him. "Of what?"

She raised her hands. "Of all the beauty around you. The trees, the snow, anything."

"I don't do landscapes." His gaze fell on her. "And I don't do models."

She snatched the camera from him. "I'm sorry. I forgot you don't take pictures of pretty things. You like it raw and ugly. Perhaps I should dig up the dead fox I buried for you."

He softly swore. "Mariella, I didn't mean it that way."

She began to walk away. "I'll see you later."

"Where are you going?"

She kept walking.

He followed her. "Mariella. Where are you going?"

"I'm continuing this walk alone. I prefer my company to yours."

"Don't go too far."

"Why not? Are you afraid there might be bears? That would be a good story for you. *Ex-model gets mauled by bear.* You could take a nice picture of me lying dead on the ground with my neck ripped away."

He grabbed her arm, his voice rough and hard. "Don't ever say that to me again."

Her gaze clashed with his. "Would you prefer me to just think it?"

His gaze fell, his grip loosening. "You don't understand."

"Then explain it to me."

"I can't take a portrait of you," he said awkwardly. "I don't do portraits."

"I'm not asking you to do my portrait. I'm asking you to take my picture as my..." Her voice died away.

His gaze lifted and he searched her eyes. "As your what?"

"I don't know."

"Yes, you do."

"I'm cold. I'm going back."

He blocked her. "You weren't cold a minute ago."

"Well, I'm cold now."

"No, you're afraid now."

She sent him a hard look. "And you're not? You can't even take a photograph of a woman standing two feet away from you. Did your father's brilliance paralyze you that much?"

A muscle in his jaw twitched. He held out his hand. "Give me the camera."

She did. "Where do you want me?"

He looked at her with interest. "Seriously?"

"To pose," she clarified.

"Oh." He shrugged. "Anywhere."

"Okay." She turned and spotted a stump surrounded by rocks. She dusted off snow. "Here's a good spot."

"Yes." He lifted the camera then didn't move. He remained frozen. Mariella stayed the same as she watched him unmoving with his trigger finger trembling above the shutter button. She didn't know what to say or whether she should move. She thought about how easy it had been for Jeremiah to take her photographs and how Ian seemed to be in agony. Why? Why would something so simple prove so painful?

"The light's dimming," she said in a bright voice. "You're right, it's not a good time to take my picture."

Ian lowered the camera and stared down at it. "You know he was brilliant with this thing. He could turn anything into art. He could take a picture of anyone and make them look beautiful.

He had an eye, a special gift. I never told him how much I—" He took a deep shuddering breath. "I'm a fraud. I went into photojournalism because I couldn't stand the comparison. I couldn't take photos like he did. Give me action, give me a stranger, but I can't take pictures of people I…" He shook his head. "Every time I tried it was never good enough. Not up to his standards." He captured her eyes. "I can't take you comparing a picture he took of you with one of mine."

"But I wouldn't."

"Perhaps, but I would and then I'd remember that you were his…model."

"Well, you need to learn to forget that." She lifted the camera in his hands. "Am I in the frame?"

"What?"

"Am I in the frame?"

He checked. "Yes."

"Good." She pressed his finger over the shutter button. "There. All done. Now let's get a few things clear. I'm *your* lover. I wasn't your father's. That's a big difference and if you can't get that straightened out we should end things now." She took the camera and turned. "I'll be back."

"Where are you going?"

"I'm giving you time to think."

"I don't need to think."

"It's good for you. I'll be back in twenty minutes."

"Make it ten, it's getting dark."

"Fifteen." She turned and winked. "It's not that dark."

"Ten. It soon will be."

Mariella playfully stuck out her tongue then left. Ian watched her, his heart feeling both heavy and light at the same time. On one hand he didn't understand her, but on another he understood her completely. He had to let the ghost of his father go if he wanted this to work. And he desperately wanted it to. She was the key to his peace; she could keep the dark shadows away. He knew that the first moment he met her. She had forced him to *feel*. He didn't even miss his darkroom. But could their relationship handle their return to New York: the innuendos, the gossip, the attention, the disbelief. How could he protect her from that? He'd have to do his best to make sure everything worked.

He returned to the cottage and saw a second car in the driveway. His heart fell. He didn't have to wait to go to New York. New York had come to them.

Chapter 15

Josh jumped out of the car. "There you are. We were getting worried."

Ian frowned, shoving his hands in his coat. "We?"

"Yes, Gen's in the car." He lowered his voice. "You wouldn't believe how much time I've been able to spend with Gen since Mariella's been away. A couple more weeks and I'm going to seal the deal."

"Seal the deal?"

"Ask her to marry me."

"Good for you," Ian said, a little envious that his brother's love life was going more smoothly than his own.

Gen stepped out of the car and shyly smiled at him. "Hi."

He waved.

Josh nudged him. "You could at least say something more. She'll be part of the family soon."

"I'm not in the mood," he grumbled.

"You could try."

"I am trying."

Gen looked at the two men unsure of what they were whispering. "Is Mariella inside?"

"No," Ian said. "She went for a walk."

"Oh."

"Come on, let me help you with the bags."

Ian helped them with their luggage and entered the house. "One room or two?" he asked at the top of the stairs.

"One," Josh said.

"Two," Gen said, then blushed.

Ian raised a brow. "Which one is it?"

"One," Josh said.

Ian nodded and showed them a spacious bedroom. While they settled in Ian cleared up the family room where he and Mariella had been staying. When Josh and Gen came downstairs he led them into the formal living room.

Josh fell into a chair. "I'm sorry we couldn't get here earlier. The crew will arrive tomorrow. You don't know how much we struggled to get here, but the thought of you alone another day with that she-wolf made me determined."

"Mariella is not a she-wolf," Gen said.

"We pictured you at each other's throats. It must have been hell."

Ian glanced out the window at the gathering darkness. "Hmm."

"This place is pretty cozy," Josh said, eager to fill the silence his brother left.

"Yes," Gen agreed. "When do you think Mariella will be back?"

Ian kept his gaze on the window and said in a flat voice, "She was supposed to have been back by now."

Gen sat on the edge of the seat. "Do you think something's happened to her?"

"I'm sure she's fine," Josh said. "That woman could scare off a grizzly bear."

"Josh, stop joking."

"I wasn't."

Gen's tone became anxious. "Should we go look for her?"

Ian didn't respond, he barely heard her. He kept thinking of a dusty day in Gambia when Cathleen wouldn't listen. She never listened to him. He'd loved her for her independence, but it was her stubbornness that had gotten her killed. He wasn't going to go through that again. He wasn't going to suffer through the constant worry, being unsure.

He wasn't going to allow another woman to rip his heart out again. He didn't move. He wouldn't think of the dangers she could face. At that moment he decided that when she walked through that door it was over between them.

But no matter what he told himself, as the minutes passed his anxiety grew. Flashes of Cathleen assaulted his thoughts, flashes of the dead fox soon joined them. He sat there thinking and waiting until it became unbearable. He jumped to his feet and grabbed his coat.

"You're going to look for her?" Gen said.

"I'm going to wring her neck." He flung open the front door with such force it banged against the wall. He walked a few feet then saw Mariella coming toward him. She smiled and waved until she saw the look on his face. Her smile fell.

"What's wrong?"

"I told you to be back in ten minutes," he said, a little too quiet.

His quiet tone didn't fool her, his gaze blazed with a scorching fury she didn't understand. "I know but—"

"You said you'd be back in fifteen."

"I know but—"

"It's forty-five minutes later."

"Yes, but I had to take this picture—"

He grabbed her arms and shook her, his voice raw with emotion. "You're not going to do this to me. Do you understand? I'm not going to let you." He shook her again. "You're arrogant, and spoiled, and stubborn and you don't care about anyone but yourself. Well, you can stay to yourself because I certainly don't want you." He abruptly released her and spun away, ignoring her when she called out his name. "You had to have your way. Do you know what could have happened out there? I do." He turned to her, the fury in his gaze almost tangible. "I know because I imagined every gruesome thing and…" He clenched his hands into fists, his voice trembling with anguish. "Damn you. Damn you for making me worry like that again."

He pressed his fists to his eyes. "I should have known better." His hands fell. "Damn it, I did. But I didn't care." He paced in front of her like a tortured caged animal. "I do now. I was a fool. I'm ready to admit it. I thought I saw something in you. It's not your fault," he said, his voice weary. "I'm glad this happened because now it's over. We had a good time, but now that's in the past. When we return to New York you'll have your life and I'll have mine."

"Ian—"

"I can't be your lover or your friend or even a distant acquaintance. I want you to forget about me and I'll do the same." He turned and marched to the house. Mariella stood there, stunned. What had she done? She was only a few minutes late. She hadn't intentionally meant to worry him. But his pain gripped her as if they were of one body and that's when she knew she loved him. There was no denying it. She loved this man who in a few short days had taken precedence in her heart and mind. The thought terrified her that he had such power, but she was strong enough to face it. And she didn't want to lose him.

For the first time in her life, she really didn't know what to say. "That's impossible. I can't forget about you."

Ian kept walking.

"Please don't do this to me. I'm sorry." When he didn't stop walking she ran up to him and grabbed his arm. "Please, Ian. I'm sorry. I should have come back sooner. You were right. I was being selfish, I was taking pictures and lost track of time and then darkness fell and for a moment I didn't know my way. It would have served me right to have gotten lost and frozen out there." She flashed a rueful smile he didn't return. "I can be stubborn for no reason and I do have a hard time admitting when I'm wrong. But I'm willing to admit it now, because you…" She took a deep breath, feeling a little ill, knowing the risk she was taking to reveal herself to him. "Because you mean a lot to me."

Ian shook his head in disbelief. "Don't do this."

Mariella cupped his chin, forcing him to look at her. "I mean it. I'm sorry. I won't do that to you again. You're right—what I did was selfish, irresponsible and inconsiderate." Fear twisted her gut that he could walk away from her; he could leave her and there was nothing she could do. She couldn't frighten him or bully him or worse yet, control him. She'd be forced to let him go and that scared her more than the depth of feelings she had for him. She tentatively touched his cheek as she would a dangerous, skittish creature and nearly wept with relief when he didn't pull away. "Please forgive me."

He closed his eyes and whispered her name. She threw her arms around him and wanted to say *I love you so much,* but kissed him instead. After a few moments he pulled away then wrapped an arm around her shoulder. "Let's go inside and get you warmed up."

"So you forgive me?"

"I'm still thinking about it."

She laughed, feeling her heart lift. "Thank you."

He playfully wrapped his arm around her neck. "You're welcome." Mariella was too taken with the moment to recognize another car in the driveway.

The moment they walked through the door, Gen rushed up to them, pushed Ian aside and gave Mariella a fierce hug.

"I was so worried," she said.

"So was I for a moment," Mariella admitted. "I'm surprised to see you here."

"We arrived about an hour ago."

"Oh."

She allowed Ian to take off her jacket and direct her to the couch. He helped her with her boots then looked at Josh. "Go get me a blanket. At the top of the stairs is the master bedroom. Better yet bring me the down comforter."

Josh stared, amazed at the scene before him. "What?"

"I need a comforter." He stood. "Never mind. I'll get it myself."

Once Ian left the room, Josh turned to Mariella. "What the hell is going on here?"

"Was it awful?" Gen asked, settling in close to Mariella and rubbing her hands to keep them warm.

"No, we managed to get on."

Josh blinked. "But Ian—" He stopped when his brother returned to the room. He watched with sickening surprise how his brother gently wrapped the comforter around Mariella. He jumped to his feet. "What the hell is going on?"

Gen tried to pull him down. "Calm down."

"Calm down?" he repeated. He stood in front of his brother. "What is all this?" He gestured to the pair. "Why are you acting this way? You hate her and she hates you—that's the way it's supposed to be."

Ian sat next to Mariella, resting his arm behind her head. "Well, that's not the way it is."

"But she was Dad's—"

Ian's gaze hardened. "She's my woman now, so I'd suggest you watch what you say."

"But Mom—"

"I'll deal with Mom."

Mariella felt the tension between the brothers and moved to leave. "Gen, let's see what we can find for dinner."

Ian kept her still. "You need to warm up first."

"I feel much better."

Josh pushed his hands through his hair then started toward the front entrance. "There are some parts of the project we need to discuss. I left my notes in the car."

Ian flashed him a bored look. "So go get them."

Mariella nudged him. "He wants to talk to you."

"He knows how to do that now."

"Ian."

He slowly stood. "Fine."

Josh walked out the door. Ian followed then stopped in the doorway and turned to her. "You know what this talk is about, don't you?"

"Yes."

"You're already causing me trouble."

"Trouble can be fun."

He winked then left and shut the door. Gen stared at Mariella, stunned. "I can't believe it."

"I know."

"You and *Ian?*"

Mariella changed the subject. Their relationship was too fragile to stand up to scrutiny. "And I noticed that you and Josh came alone."

Gen blushed.

"Have you told him about—?"

"I will."

"When?"

Gen sighed. "Soon."

"We both know there are no notes there," Ian said as Josh marched to his car.

Josh stopped then slowly spun on his heel. He gestured to the house. "This is about Dad, isn't it?"

"No, it's not."

"Yes, it is. You want to get your last leg in."

"You don't know what you're talking about."

"And you don't know what the hell you're doing. That woman is trouble. Don't you know that? Try to think with your brain. That trouble in Georgia is just the tip of the iceberg. You know that lady is suing, right? And if you don't think that's bad enough think about how the papers are going to run with this story." He threw up his hands and stared up at the sky. "Of all the women in the world you've got to go for your dead father's mistress."

"She wasn't—"

"She's got you believing that bull? As if that's not bad enough she's making you soft."

"Look—"

"Did you see the way you acted just a moment ago? I'm telling you she's slowly snipping off your balls and she'll trap you just like she trapped Dad."

Ian shook his head. "You don't know her."

"Maybe, but I know you and I don't want to sit by and watch you make another mistake."

Ian stilled. "What do you mean by that?"

"You know what I mean. Marrying Cathleen was a mistake. You wanted to be different from Dad so you married a plain, ordinary woman who liked to take pictures of everything our father was against. And you married her and found out that she was selfish and conniving. I know that she used you."

Ian kept his voice neutral. "No, she didn't."

"She used you to get certain assignments. She used your connections to further her career. Come on, Ian, you know she used you."

Ian grabbed Josh by the collar and shoved him against the car. "No, she loved me and I loved her. You don't know—"

Josh's gaze clashed with his. "I know that she took some of your photos and passed them off as hers."

Ian shook his head as though trying to rid the words from his mind. "It wasn't like that."

"You were blind because you thought she was different than the many women who came in and out of your life. But Cathleen was just the same as the others. We all saw it, Dad, Mom and I, and we felt sorry for you. When she died…"

Ian released his grip. "You were glad?" he said flatly, all strength leaving him.

"No, we didn't expect it to affect you that much."

"She was a great photojournalist."

"But you were better. That's probably why she took more and more dangerous assignments because she knew she wasn't that good. Face it Ian. She used you and Mariella is using you too."

His mouth became a thin line. "You're wrong."

Josh sighed. "No, I'm not, but I guess you'll have to find out on your own." He went back inside.

Ian pounded the hood of the car. His brother was wrong. Cathleen hadn't used him. He had let her get credit for some of his photos. They had worked so close together, after a short period he felt they were like one person. Whatever she achieved he felt he'd achieved also. Cathleen had been brilliant and fearless. She had a passion for the work. He had loved her, but he'd never been sure she felt the same. He knew Cathleen's first love was her work. She lived and breathed for it and ultimately died for it. He didn't need Mariella to love him. He didn't want to be alone anymore and he knew she was right for him.

"Where's Ian?" Mariella asked when Josh returned alone.

"He's still outside."

"Why?" She stood. "Is something wrong?"

"No. Why can't you just leave him alone?" he said when she moved toward the door.

"Don't talk like that to me."

Josh hesitated then looked at Gen and gathered his courage. "Why not? You've done enough damage."

"Damage?"

"Yes." He rested his hands on his hips and looked at her with contempt. "Since we only have a week left on this project let me tell you a few things. You're no good for him. My father was good at handling spoiled and selfish divas. He thought it was fun. But even he fell for you. He fell for you so hard that because he couldn't have you the way he wanted he ended it all. Life meant nothing to him."

Mariella grabbed her throat, aghast. "What are you talking about?"

"I'm talking about the note he left behind. I'm talking about the herbs you gave him that he used to end his life."

"No, he told me to get those for him."

"Of course. He knew you were too dumb to know what they were. What he could do with them. You toyed with him all those months."

"I never toyed with him. We were friends."

His face colored with anger. "He loved you! But you were too blind to notice. You're so used to men adoring you and wanting you that you can't tell the difference. But I did." He pounded his chest. "I never saw him look at another woman as he did when he was with you. You knew your power over him and teased him. You treated him like a boy when he wanted to be treated like a man. He knew he was old and sick and couldn't face it anymore. Now you're trying to do the same to my brother, but I won't let you."

"Shut up, Josh," Ian said from the doorway.

"I'm just telling the truth."

"You're wrong," Mariella said quietly, blinking away tears. "If your father decided to end his life, it wasn't because of me."

"Oh yeah? Dad and I may not have always seen eye to eye, but I knew him."

Ian slammed the door behind him. "Leave her alone."

"Tell her about the will."

"No."

"What about the will?" Mariella asked.

Josh began to smile. "You really want to know?"

"Shut up, Josh," Ian said.

Mariella nodded. "Yes, tell me."

"We had to put you on this project or we would lose everything. The magazine, the licenses, the house, everything. Do you know where it would go? To you. He put you above the mother of his children and his own sons. Do you still want to claim that you were just friends?"

Ian lunged at him. "I said leave her alone!"

Gen jumped to her feet and shouted, "Both of you stop it." They turned to her, shocked. "Now, I didn't know Jeremiah well, but I do know Mariella and she wouldn't have done anything to hurt him. And before you rip her apart there are a few things you need to know about me."

Mariella reached for her hand. "No, Gen, you don't have to do that now."

"Yes, I do. Josh, I met Mariella while I was walking the streets of Italy."

He shrugged. "So?"

"I was a call girl."

Chapter 16

Josh stared at her, confused. "What do you mean?"

"Exactly what I said. I was a call girl when Mariella found me. I'd been a top model when the exotic look was in, but when the trend fizzled I ended up being stranded in Italy with no money and no way back home and I fell in with a nefarious man who promised me money if I did certain things. It became my life for a while and would have been my future had Mariella not spotted me. She knew who I was immediately and I'll never forget the words she spoke to me as I was about to get in a man's car: 'I'll give you three times what he's willing to offer.'

"I took her up on her offer, explained my situation and she helped to get me my papers and money to leave. She let me live with her and gave me a job as her assistant. She changed my life. So if you want to talk about bad behavior, or having a woman in your life with a past then you should talk to me and leave Mariella alone. Excuse me." Holding back tears, Gen turned and raced up the stairs.

"But that doesn't make sense," Josh said in disbelief. "She was a top model with jobs all around the world. How could that have happened?"

"Easy." Mariella sighed. "Models are thrown away all the time and money isn't always as free-flowing as people would think. But it's not *how* it happened, it's the fact that it *did*. Can you handle that?" Mariella sent Josh a knowing look. "What would your mother and the community think if they found out about her earlier occupation?"

"I don't care."

"Don't be a hypocrite. Of course you care."

"No, that's not true. What she did in her past is just that—in the past. I don't care about that now."

"Does that apply to all women or just her?"

"Gen isn't like you. She needs someone to protect her, you don't."

Mariella folded her arms. "You're right. I know how to take care of myself. No one would think of coming to my rescue."

Ian sent her a look, but didn't reply.

"So you plan on being her protector no matter what?"

Josh nodded. "Yes, because I love her." He felt as if his heart would burst. Not from what he had heard, but the thought of Gen being used that way. He needed to be with her.

"Then she's a very lucky woman."

"No, I'm a lucky man." He raced up the stairs.

Ian shoved his hands in his pockets and looked at Mariella curious. "Why did you lie?"

She turned to him, surprised. "I didn't."

"You said no one would come to your rescue." He reached out and fingered a strand of hair on her cheek. "You know I would," he said in a voice that promised a lot more than rescue.

She swallowed, her pulse racing. "Josh wouldn't have believed that."

Ian grinned. "He isn't thinking straight right now. People in love rarely do."

"No."

He glanced at the stairs, amused. "Good thing we aren't in love, isn't it?"

Mariella wrapped the blanket tighter around her and sent a wistful glance at his profile. "Yes."

Josh opened the door to the bedroom he shared with Gen and saw her sitting on the bed. He stood in front of her. "Why didn't you tell me sooner?

Did Mariella tell you not to? You can't let her control you."

"She wanted me to tell you from the beginning," Gen said, quick to defend her friend. "She kept you away at first because she was trying to protect me."

He sat beside her. "From what?"

"From getting hurt."

"I wouldn't hurt you."

She hugged herself and turned away from Josh. "You may not mean to. But now that you know my past your opinion of me will change."

"I'm surprised," he admitted, "but I still love you. Nothing will change that."

She cautiously turned to him. "Not even your brother?"

"Not even him."

"But you were just trying to change his mind about Mariella. You can only see her one way. As the woman your father loved."

"She's different."

"She's a woman and no woman likes to be labeled. Don't judge her so harshly. She was your father's choice."

"You don't understand."

"Did she make him happy?"

"Yes, but I've dealt with women like Mariella all my life. They're out to get what they want no matter what the price and they'll make you sorry when they don't. My brother deserves better. That woman doesn't love anyone but herself."

Gen noisily cleared her throat.

"Except maybe you."

"She also has sisters."

"You're missing the point."

"No, you are. I know my friend and I know how she feels although she will never admit it."

"And I know my brother and I know she's no good for him."

"She's probably too good for him. He's bullying and opinionated."

"And she's temperamental and—" He held up his hands in surrender. "Wait, why are we fighting about them?"

"Because Mariella is a big part of my life."

"Yes, I know that. Do you know how many times I tried to get close to you and she prevented me?"

"I told you why."

"But you can understand why she's low on my list."

"Your brother isn't one of my favorite people."

"Why not?"

"I find his anger frightening."

"He's harmless—most times."

"I don't trust him and prefer to keep my distance."

Josh rubbed his chin. "That's a problem."

"Why?"

"Because if you say yes to my next question he'd be your brother-in-law."

Gen stared, taken aback by his offer. "You're asking me to marry you?"

"Yes."

"What will your mother say?"

"I'll handle Mother."

She raised a brow. "Funny, you sounded just like Ian then."

"It happens sometimes. So what do you say?"

She chewed her lip. "I don't know."

He gathered her close. "I promise if you say yes nothing anyone can say will tear us apart."

A tremulous smile touched her face as she stared at the man who held her heart. "Then the answer is yes."

Downstairs, Ian and Mariella sat in silence. Ian sat on the floor staring at the glowing flame of the fireplace while Mariella stayed curled up on the couch staring at their reflections in the mirror.

"This changes everything, doesn't it?" she finally said.

He continued to stare at the flames. "What does?"

"The fact that your father loved me."

Ian lifted a poker and jabbed a log in the fireplace.

"He's like this ghost hanging between us and there's nothing we can do."

Ian set the poker aside.

"What are you thinking?"

"I'm thinking that my father and I were alike more than I'd want to admit. We both fell in love with women who didn't feel the same about us."

"I did love him."

"But not in the way he wanted. It could have made all the difference."

"Are you going to accuse me of killing him too?"

He shook his head.

"But you were thinking it. Right?"

"No, I wasn't." He stood and turned his back to the fire. "I just realized something."

"What?"

"Unlike my father, I'm healthy, happy and I don't love you and I don't care if you love me." He sat down beside her, resting a large, solid hand on her knee. "So we have nothing to worry about."

Mariella forced a smile. "Right."

"Good."

They fell quiet again, but their silence was soon interrupted by the sound of feet racing down the staircase.

"We're getting married," Josh said, holding Gen's hand with pride.

Mariella leaped up and hugged her friend. "Congratulations."

Ian returned his gaze to the fire.

Josh let Gen's hand go and moved toward Ian, already defensive. "I don't care what you think."

Ian kept his gaze averted. "You don't know what I think."

"Yes, I do. You think she's after my money. Dad thought the same thing."

"That's not what I'm thinking." Ian sent Josh a sharp look. "But you're afraid others might."

"Give me some credit. You know I don't care what anyone else thinks."

"Congratulations then." Ian stood and gave his brother a slap on the back then motioned to the kitchen. "Let's find something to eat."

The next day Josh contacted the crew and models scheduled for the Vermont shoot to make arrangements to get back on schedule. Everything was to be shot on the property, which had a magnificent view of a valley, a large pond with an array of ducks and geese, a housekeeper's cottage and a beautiful sculptured topiary garden. Following a hearty lunch, complemented with food that Josh and Gen had purchased, the four parted into pairs. Gen and Josh went for a long walk while Mariella occupied her time taking additional pictures. Ian took a nap.

Mariella returned and found him sleeping with his shirt halfway open, not surprised that even his undershirt was black. Even in sleep he looked dark and alone, but that wasn't right. He'd invited her to be a part of his life, right? But only part; there was still another part she couldn't reach.

His eyes fluttered open. When he saw her he flashed a slow sexy smile. "Enjoy yourself?"

She lifted her camera and took a picture of him then returned his smile. "Definitely."

The photo shoot in Vermont went somewhat smoothly. Mariella did not complain about the selection of models, but she did get into a shouting match with one who decided to argue with her about the clothes. She fired her on the spot; Ian didn't intervene. The crew followed instructions without hassle although Mariella frustrated the makeup artist, Jennifer and the remaining models, with her rigid requirement for a particular look. She wanted stark and artistic. Jennifer tried, but each time Mariella yelled, "More. More. I want more! Do I have to do the makeup myself?"

Jennifer didn't reply though it was clear what she thought of her. Everyone was thrilled once the shoot was over. But Mariella surprised everyone when she told them what an outstanding job they'd done and she specifically told Jennifer that she would go far in the industry and she hoped to work with her again.

Josh, Gen, Mariella and Ian stayed an extra day after everyone returned to New York. The evening before they left, Gen found Ian out back staring at Mariella in the distance as she took more pictures.

Gen cautiously approached him. "Hi."

"Hi," he said then pointed. "Mariella has taken over one hundred pictures of that sunset. Each time it looks the same to me, but she sees something different."

"Yes. Mariella can be like that." She cleared her throat. "I want you to know something."

"I'm not in the mood for more secrets."

"It's not that."

"Good, then what is it?"

"I love Josh. I'll deal with what others think of us, but I do care what you think."

He nodded.

She shifted awkwardly, feeling uneasy with his silence. "Do you believe me?"

He folded his arms. "I want to. For now you are keeping him happy. I'll believe you in a couple of years."

"Years?"

The ghost of a smile touched his lips. "It will go by faster than you think."

She narrowed her eyes in accusation. "Are you teasing me?"

"Of course I am."

"That wasn't very nice."

"We're going to be family soon, you'd better get used to me."

"I don't think that's possible."

A snowball hit him in the shoulder before he could reply.

He looked up and saw Mariella. "What was that for?"

"You're such an easy target."

He bent down and gathered snow. "Is that right?"

She took a step back. "You can't hit me—I'm holding a very expensive camera."

"I won't be aiming at the camera."

Mariella saw the look in his eye and took another step back. "Now, Ian, be fair."

He raised his hand. She set the camera down and ran. Ian ran after her.

Josh walked up behind Gen. "What's going on?" he asked as Ian hit Mariella in the back with his snowball. She in turn scooped up snow and splashed him. He grabbed her and they both stumbled to the ground.

Gen smiled. "They're falling in love."

Ian was glad to return back to New York and was prepared to enter the quiet of his house. Josh had told him that while he was away their mother and Otis had gotten back together. He opened the door ready to greet Sylvester, but when he did, he saw that Sylvester wasn't alone.

"Lily," he bellowed.

His housekeeper rushed up to him. "Yes, Mr. Cooper?"

"Where is she?"

"Who?"

"My mother."

"I thought your brother told you. She is back with Mr. Fassel."

"Then what is that?" He pointed to Candy who was circling around him, excited by his return.

"She said that Candy and Sylvester got on so well she didn't want to separate them and she's had her eye on getting a—"

"I don't care." He looked at Candy. "Stop."

The little dog immediately sat on her hind legs and stared up at him, dressed in a turquoise cashmere sweater.

Ian glanced at Sylvester. "You're supposed to guard the fortress. What have you done?"

"They're really cute together," Lily said.

Ian glared at her.

She grabbed his suitcase. "I'll just take this to your room."

"Thank you." Ian stormed into his study and picked up the phone. He started to dial his mother's number then stopped. Instead he dialed Mariella, "How would you like a dog?" he said.

Chapter 17

Two hours later, Mariella sat in Ian's study and they both stared at Sylvester and Candy, who lay together on the rug.

"You could keep her," Mariella said.

"Keep her? Look at me. Do I look like the kind of guy who would own a Chihuahua that has more clothes than I do?"

"I would take her but my schedule can be hectic."

"So take her with you. She's small enough to fit in your makeup case."

"Yes, but if I took her Sylvester would be lonely."

"He's got me."

"You're not the same."

"Hmm."

"Think about it."

"I'm not dressing her. Lily will have to do that."

After the Candy incident Ian thought his problems were over but when Mariella learned that the photos had already been sent to the layout designer, she demanded to be part of the selection process. Ian refused and after a heated debate she had to admit defeat. The winter holiday season arrived. Gen and Josh went to Colorado together and though Mariella invited Ian to spend time with her family he declined.

Mariella tried to convince him otherwise, not wanting to admit how much she'd miss him, but he wouldn't budge so she was forced to leave him. Ian liked to be alone at the holidays. Or at least he used to be. When New Year's Eve came, Ian sat all alone in his family room in front of the TV with just Sylvester and Candy. He wished he'd taken Mariella's offer. "Next year will be different."

He was about to open his second can of beer when the doorbell rang. "Who is it?" he called.

"Mariella."

"Who?" he said, not sure he'd heard correctly.

"Mariella."

He couldn't open the door fast enough and twice fumbled with the lock. When he finally got the door open he saw Mariella holding a large box.

"What is that?"

"Don't ask, just help me with it."

He took it from her. "Is this my lump of coal?"

She laughed. "No, take it into the kitchen."

He did then pulled her in his arms and kissed her hello. "Now tell me what this is."

She opened the box and pulled out containers of food. "Isabella made grilled chicken, Gabby made whipped sweet potatoes, Daniella made asparagus with cheese sauce and I made the pumpkin pie."

He picked up the pie. "Then I'll have to try this first."

"You're lucky I was able to get you a slice. It is delicious."

He grinned. "I admire your modesty."

"Personally I find modesty an accepted form of lying. So what did you buy me?"

"For what?"

"You didn't buy me anything?"

"I'll take you shopping tomorrow."

"Good." She handed him another box. "Here's your gift."

"Is it a shirt?"

"No."

"A tie?"

"No, just open it."

He ripped open the box and pulled out an antique camera.

"Do you like it?" Mariella asked anxiously when he continued to just stare at it. "My sister Isabella helped me select it."

"It's beautiful. I just have to think of the right place to put it."

Mariella had no problem directing him where it would best be displayed. She decided that a shelf in his study was best. Ian didn't argue. He just told her to retrieve a letter from his desk. She did and noticed it had her name on it. She discovered that it contained a coupon for a week's pass at an exclusive spa. Mariella thanked him in the best way she could think of and they welcomed in the New Year in each other's arms.

In the following weeks, they were careful not to be seen too much together although some papers had already hinted at their relationship with such titles as "Guess Who's Turning Over in His Grave?" and "Family Portrait." They turned heads everywhere they went, sometimes because people knew who they were, other times because people couldn't help staring at such a striking pair. Ian got used to the attention, very aware of how Mariella commanded people's attention, especially men. Although he nearly broke the face of a photographer who took a picture of them as they left a movie theater. Mariella persuaded him not to.

Mariella was too content with her life to worry
about what the papers said. Her relationship with
Ian continued to grow and only a few weeks after
returning to New York she'd been commissioned
for a book project and magazine work. Ian kept
busy with *Flash* and the upcoming gallery event
in spring. He helped Mariella with her craft and
they spent time together in his darkroom and on
his computer. They would take excursions out of
the city and photograph whatever interested them,
then go home and critique their efforts. All was
well except Ian's occasional calls from Shirley.

"Do you know what people are saying?" she
demanded.

"Yes, Mom." He glanced over at Mariella who
sat in his study buttoning up Candy's sweater.

"Some think you're fulfilling an Oedipus desire."

"Don't be disgusting."

"I don't approve of this. I hope you're still not
thinking of marrying her."

"Bye, Mom." He hung up the phone and stared
at Mariella. That was exactly what he planned to
do, but he'd ask her at the right time.

In February, Yolanda and her family came to
visit Ian. Mariella was excited to see them and
invited the family to dinner at her place. The next
day she took the two girls shopping and gave them
tips on how to select fabric, look for tailored
pieces and what not to buy. While Tatiana showed

her enthusiasm, Hannah looked bored. Even when Mariella tried to show them makeup tips, Hannah preferred to search the apartment for a missing earring. She wasn't sorry to be dropped off at her parents' hotel.

Mariella's relationship with Ian progressed more smoothly. They spent much of their time traveling to museums and galleries. On one weekend, Ian called Mariella and told her to pack a bag for at least two nights. He picked her up and drove to Washington, D.C., where they visited several museums including the Spy Museum and the National Gallery of Art. All too soon winter turned into spring and Mariella decided to visit her sister Isabella in upstate New York.

"Are you sure you don't mind me coming?" Ian asked.

"No, I want you to meet them."

Ian could gauge the distance to the house by the excitement on Mariella's face. He was better able to read her moods these days. Someone else would see a cool woman in a sports jacket and jeans, but he saw the slight softening of her mouth and the brightness of her eyes. She looked like a young girl on a trip to a fantasy land. He hid a smile. "You're really happy about this. But you saw your sister in December."

"I know, but I never tire of seeing them. I can't wait to surprise her."

Ian looked at her, alarmed. "She doesn't know you're coming?"

"No."

"She might not be home."

"She'll be home. She would have just finished playing the piano for Nicodemus."

"Nicodemus?"

"Yes."

Before he could ask more questions she said, "Turn here."

He did and was soon greeted by the sight of a large Victorian house. He parked and Mariella jumped out of the car and raced up the stairs then stopped and stood in front of the door.

Ian slowly climbed the stairs, sending her an odd look. "Why won't you knock?"

"Hear that piano?"

He nodded, the melodious sound coming through the open window.

"I don't want to disturb her. She'll be done in a minute."

"But—"

"Nicodemus doesn't like it when a song doesn't reach the end." She tilted her head and listened. "There's the last note." She raised her hand and knocked. Moments later a petite woman answered. Her eyes widened and she threw herself at Mariella as though she hadn't seen her in years.

"Mariella!" she said, her slender arms wrapped

around her sister in a big hug. She stepped back. "I can't believe you're here. It's so good to see you."

"It's good to see you too."

The woman directed her bright brown eyes on Ian. "And who might you be?"

Mariella turned to him. "This is Ian Cooper."

She shook his hand. "Yes, I know. I was only being polite." Although Isabella didn't have her sister's exquisite beauty, she was captivating and her intelligent, assessing gaze made heat steal into his cheeks.

He released her hand. "It's a pleasure to meet you."

"Thank you."

"You play the piano beautifully."

"Hmm." She turned and looked down at the white cat who sat in the middle of the hallway. "Tell that to him."

Ian looked around. "To who?"

She pointed at the cat. "Nicodemus."

"You play for a cat?"

Isabella raised a finger to her lips. "Shh, I'm not always sure that he is one."

Ian sent Mariella a curious look, but she just grinned. The cat looked up at them, then walked past and out the door.

"Don't ask, come on in."

"Where's Kati?" Mariella asked.

"Out with her dad. They'll be back soon." She

looped her arm through Mariella's. "Now you have to tell me all that you've been up to."

Ian followed the pair into the living room, but they talked so fast he couldn't catch what they were saying. Instead he looked around the house at the pictures on the wall. He saw four young women in front of Big Ben and the Houses of Parliament. Another photograph was of a young woman who looked like a chubby version of Mariella, an older man and two small children. He spotted some other pictures of Mariella and her three sisters with their father. What he found curious was that in most of the pictures, Mariella was either on her father's lap or at his side. Mariella was as exquisite then as she was now, but looked a lot happier as though the world was her private playground. Interestingly Ian didn't see that happy girl in later pictures. It was as if that little girl was taken away after the death of her father.

Ian turned when he heard the front door close.

"Alex," Isabella called. "We have visitors."

"Who?"

"Mariella and Ian. Ian's around here somewhere. I'm afraid we made him feel a bit excluded."

Ian knew that was his cue to emerge from the hallway. He walked into the room and saw a tall, strikingly handsome young man holding a little girl. The little girl had the Duvall look—her features both broad and fine, clear brown eyes surrounded by a perfect row of curled lashes.

Isabella rushed up to him and pulled him forward. He was too stunned by her boldness to refuse. "Alex, this is Ian Cooper. Ian, my husband Alex."

They shook hands.

"And this is Kati."

Ian went to shake her hand, but she moved away, and hugged her father's neck. "She takes a while to warm up to people," Alex said.

Ian shrugged. "That's okay."

"Cooper, your name sounds familiar to me. Were you the one who did that feature story in *Time* about the condition of Aborigines in Australia?"

"That was a while back, but yes, that was me."

"Impressive piece of journalism. It actually encouraged people to see if they could help make a difference. They're developing schools in the area from what I understand."

"Yes, you're right."

Alex sat down, placing Kati on his lap. "What are you working on now?"

"Nothing."

Mariella filled in for him. "He is the owner of *Flash* magazine."

Alex nodded. "Oh."

Ian saw some of his interest dim and sighed. He saw the little girl wiggle off her father's lap then find her doll in the corner and start to talk to it. "It started out as my father's company," he said, feeling the need to explain.

"Really," Alex said with renewed interest. "And you took over?"

"Yes, he asked me to."

"He must be proud."

"He's dead."

"Oh. I'm sorry."

Isabella hit him in the arm. "I told you that."

Alex rubbed his arm. "I forgot."

"You weren't listening."

He grinned. "Yes, that too."

Mariella spoke up. "His father was Jeremiah Cooper, the renowned photographer. But of course I wouldn't have expected you to know him."

Alex raised a brow. "Because I just have money, but no class?"

"Exactly."

"Do you want me to share what I think about you?"

"Alex," Isabella said in warning.

"Please do," Mariella said. "Enlighten me." She crossed her legs and leaned forward. "I always find it fascinating to know what thoughts you manage to put together when you're not busy hammering something."

"I enjoy hammering. I just pretend I'm closing your mouth."

"Stop it, you two," Isabella said. "You're making Ian nervous. He doesn't know you're joking."

Alex looked at Mariella. "Are we joking?"

Mariella checked her manicure. "I was being serious. I think you're uncouth."

"And I think you're a spoiled brat."

Ian watched the interplay of teasing with fascination. He'd never experienced such banter in his own family. His family used cutting remarks and put-downs when they spoke to each other. "How long have you known Mariella?"

"Too long."

Isabella hit him. "Alex, stop it."

"You're going to leave me with bruises."

"Then behave yourself."

"I'm just answering honestly."

"Careful," Mariella said in a sweet tone. "I knew you when you were still sucking on your mother's—"

Alex glared at her. "Watch it."

Isabella smiled at Ian. "Just ignore them. We basically all grew up together. And as you can see we get along famously." Isabella stood. "I'm going to call Velma. You two must stay for dinner."

They did. Not that Ian felt they had a chance to say no. He tried to be cordial though he felt a little uneasy when Alex's mother Velma arrived. The older woman watched him with suspicious eyes.

She dressed well, but had the hands of a woman who'd worked all her life. He attempted to relieve any of her suspicions by joining in, but most of the time he remained an observer as they all talked and laughed. They sat for a long time gathered around the dinner table piled high with a selection of food: jerk chicken, a pot of greens, jambalaya, done right, fried plantains and rice. During dinner there was a lively discussion between Mariella, Isabella and Alex about their other siblings. Ian was captivated by it all.

He wondered about how easy and friendly their relationship was. There didn't appear to be any competition between them. He'd always thought these happy families weren't real—that they were staged, a trick of the light. But it was clear that they all genuinely cared for each other.

They had a special bond that was real and true. Ian felt like an intruder. At that moment he wished for the sanctity of his darkroom. The joy and beauty around him was almost painful. Like someone not used to light stepping out into the sun. After dinner as everyone gathered in the conservatory, Ian slipped outside. He stared out at the backyard, still showing signs of the setting sun over the grass.

Inside, Mariella watched him.

"I'd be careful of that one," Velma said.

Mariella turned to her, surprised. "You don't like him?"

"I didn't say I don't like him, I just said be careful."

Mariella looked at Isabella. "What do you think?"

"He seems very nice."

"How do you know?" Velma countered. "He's hardly said anything."

Alex who'd been quietly watching the exchange spoke up. "I don't think it's fair to pull the poor guy to shreds in his absence. He didn't come to get analyzed."

Isabella smiled at her husband then blew him a kiss. "I love you. You're still so young and innocent."

He frowned. "What do you mean?"

"Why else would Mariella have brought him here?"

Alex looked blank then began to understand. "Oh."

"So what do you think?"

He leaned forward, resting his elbows on his knees. "Well, I think he's a good guy except for one thing."

"What?"

"I question his taste in women."

Isabella picked up a couch pillow and threw it at him. "Go away."

He stood up and laughed. "With pleasure."

Once Alex had left the room, the women resumed their discussion. "It isn't about what we think, dear," Velma said. "It's what you think."

"She loves him," Isabella said. "It's obvious to me."

Velma looked grim. "Then you've chosen one strange man to fall in love with. I'm not saying there's anything clearly wrong with him. He's attractive."

"He's *gorgeous,*" Isabella said.

"Hey!" a male voice said from the hallway.

"Alex, stop listening in or I'll describe in detail just how gorgeous I think he is."

Alex stuck his head inside. "Go ahead."

"Stop it," Mariella said. "Let Velma finish what she was saying."

Isabella nodded. "You're right, go ahead, Velma."

Velma straightened. "Yes, even though he's attractive, and successful you must understand that you do not marry *that* man."

Isabella glanced at Mariella, confused. "What do you mean?"

"I mean that you can marry a man who is loyal to his employees and disloyal to his wife. A man who is attractive to the world and ugly to his family. Mariella, if you are in love with this man I hope you've fallen in love with the *man* and not just the image he gives you. Because he seems the type of man who is adept at showing the right image."

"People misunderstand him. He really is kind

and smart and…you remember those pictures of children that I have over my bed? He took those pictures when he was younger."

Velma took her hand. "Yes, but that was when he was younger. What is he like now?"

Isabella jumped to her feet. "I've got an idea."

The two women looked at her. "What?"

"Kati and I are going to go for a walk."

Chapter 18

Outside, Ian stood mesmerized by the sight of a family of rabbits. He didn't hear Isabella at the door until she spoke. "Hi."

"Hi," he said, noticing that she held Kati's hand.

"We're going for a walk to take some pictures," she said, gesturing to the camera in her other hand. "Dad used to do that with us all the time. You might like it. Would you like to come?"

"No thanks."

She sent him a considering look then rubbed her arms. "Brr, it's a little colder than I thought." She quickly retreated inside. "I'd better go get a jacket. Could you just watch her for a moment?

I'll be back in a second." She handed him the camera, then dashed back inside before he could reply.

Ian looked down at Kati, who stood desolate on the porch. She looked up at him, her eyes filling with tears. Then her face crumpled up.

Dread gripped him. "No, please don't do this to me."

She let out a big wail.

Ian looked helplessly at the closed door. "Mommy's coming back. Don't cry." He knelt down in front of her. "Please don't cry."

She didn't hear him, filling up her little lungs for another wail.

He lifted the camera. "Would you like me to take your picture? Huh? I'll take your picture so you can be like Aunt Mariella?"

The name of her aunt seemed to catch her attention. Her crying immediately stopped, becoming sniffles.

He waved the camera. "Do you want your picture taken?"

She pointed to it. "Picwur," she said. Although her pronunciation wasn't accurate, Ian knew exactly what she meant.

Ian let out a sigh of relief. "Yes, let me take your picture." He lifted up the camera and looked at her through the LCD monitor. Without any direction Kati placed her hands on her hips, posed and smiled.

He grinned, then snapped the photo. "You like getting your picture taken, don't you?" He turned the screen to her so that she could see her image. She giggled.

At that moment Isabella appeared. "I'm sorry. Her jacket was buried in the closet." She took Kati's hand. "Come on, poppet."

Kati defiantly yanked her hand away. "No."

Isabella rolled her eyes. "They weren't kidding you about the terrible twos." She took her daughter's hand again. "Come on."

Kati tried to yank her hand free again. When she couldn't she began to cry. "Picwur, picwur."

Isabella stared down at her at a loss. "What?"

"She wants her picture taken," Ian said.

"Of course you would, you vain little thing. All right." She gave Ian a knowing look.

Soon Kati was all smiles again. She ran in front of Ian and took a striking pose looking out from behind an evergreen. Ian looked at Isabella and shrugged.

"Go ahead. As you have discovered, she loves having her picture taken."

He did. "She's beautiful."

"Shh, we're trying to keep it a secret from her."

Ian laughed as Kati struck another pose. "I think she already knows."

"She loves fashion and pictures of her Aunt Ma-La-La. She hasn't gotten 'Mariella' down yet."

Ian took more pictures of her playing in the

front lawn picking up buttercups then throwing them up in the air and laughing when they fell on her face, falling back on the ground and twirling around, her joy contagious.

From a distance Mariella and Velma watched them.

"I suppose he has possibilities," Velma said, watching Ian tuck the bouquet of buttercups Kati had given him in his jacket pocket.

"Yes," Mariella said softly. "I think so."

Kati glanced up. When she saw Mariella, she ran over to her and grabbed her hand then pointed at Ian. "Picwur. Picwur."

Mariella lifted Kati up in her arms. "That sounds like fun." She winked at Ian. "Can you manage two beautiful people?"

He clicked the shutter button. "I'll do my best."

For the next half hour, he took pictures of Mariella with Kati and some with Isabella, although she preferred not to be in the picture. When he had finished, Ian knelt next to Kati, who had been standing patiently to see herself and showed her all the pictures.

"You're amazing," Isabella said next to him. "These are very good."

"You could send these to a modeling agency," Mariella said.

"Kati is not going to model."

Mariella shrugged, unperturbed. "Just a thought."

"But I definitely have to have them framed. They're works of art."

"More, more," Kati demanded.

Isabella shook her head. "No more. That's enough now."

"No. I want picwurs!"

"We are going to go inside." Isabella bent down until she was at eye level with Kati. "Now."

Kati scrunched up her face, tears building in her eyes.

"And if you cry, I'll tell Aunt Mariella not to tuck you in."

Kati folded her arms then marched into the house. Isabella watched her, shaking her head, then looked at her sister. "Does she remind you of anyone?"

Mariella feigned innocence. "I don't know what you mean."

Ian grinned. "I do."

Moments later, he was sitting in the living room trying to blend into the background as Velma, Mariella and Isabella talked in the kitchen when Kati came up to him with a ribbon and brush then turned and sat down in front of him. He stared down at her perplexed; when he didn't move she looked up at him and smiled and said, "Make me pwitti."

He still wasn't sure what that meant, but when Alex came in and saw them he explained. "She wants you to put the ribbon in her hair."

Ian shook his head. "Go ask your mommy."

She frowned. "No."

Ian glanced at Alex. "She really likes that word."

"Yes," Alex said. "But the ribbon means she likes you."

"But I don't know how to put a ribbon in a little girl's hair."

"She doesn't care. I do it wrong all the time."

Ian scratched his head then said, "You're going to regret this, little one." He pulled up her braids and wrapped them in a bow. "There. You're done."

She jumped up to her feet. "Daddy, I'm pwitti."

"Yes, you are."

She skipped out of the room announcing how pretty she was.

Alex laughed. "We'll tell her about having a good personality later."

Isabella came into the room holding Kati's hand, with Mariella behind her. She looked at Alex surprised. "Did you do this?"

Alex shook his head then pointed to Ian. "He did."

Ian moved uncomfortably. "She asked me to."

"I'm impressed," Isabella said. "She looks lovely, where did you learn to do that?"

"Watching my mother with Candy."

"Candy?"

"Yes, uh…a close friend of hers. She likes to

do her hair all the time and I guess I picked up a few things."

Isabella jerked a finger at her husband. "Perhaps you could teach him something. Every time she goes to Alex she ends up looking like a madwoman."

"I do my best," Alex said. "I'm not good with hair, but give me a good piece of wood and I can work miracles."

"Yes, well it's time she goes to bed."

To everyone's surprise, Kati didn't protest. Instead she grabbed Ian's and Mariella's hands, determined that they would tuck her in.

They obliged and took her to her room. Kati jumped into bed and fell back. Ian stared at Mariella hoping to follow her lead; fortunately she knew exactly what to do and even listened to an unintelligible story Kati shared with her. When Kati glanced at him he managed a smile that seemed to satisfy her because she turned on her side and went to sleep.

After tea and dessert, Ian and Mariella headed back to the city. Alex and Isabella stood on the porch and watched their car disappear.

"What did you really think of him?" Isabella said.

Alex wrapped an arm around her waist. "He seems nice, but he didn't say much."

She rested her head on his shoulder. "Did you notice the way he looked at her?"

"That look of terror is normal."

"He didn't look at her that way." She pinched him. "Be serious."

He rubbed his side. "How do you think he looked at her?"

Isabella was quiet a moment then said softly, "As though he'd finally found something he was looking for."

"I'm exhausted," Mariella said, opening her front door.

Ian fell on the couch. "It's a longer drive than you'd think."

She leaned over and kissed him on the cheek. "Thanks for coming with me."

"You're welcome."

"And thanks for the pictures."

"I'm glad you liked them."

"I loved them." She stood and pulled off her blouse. "I'm tired." She unhooked her bra and grinned at him. "Could you tuck me in?"

Ian stood. "Certainly, little girl."

She placed her bra around his shoulders and pulled him toward the bedroom. "Do you promise to tuck me in nice and tight?"

"Definitely."

"And make sure that I'm safe and warm?"

He lifted her in his arms and walked into the bedroom. "Absolutely," he said, placing her on the bed.

She undid his shirt. "And you'll check for any monsters under the bed?"

"Yes."

She pulled his shirt off. "And in the closet?"

"Yes."

She pressed her lips against his. "Good."

"Now there's something I want to ask you," Ian said, thinking this was the best time to ask her to marry him.

She brought him close and arched her pelvis toward him. "Ask me in the morning."

He immediately responded. "But—"

"I'm not in the mood to talk."

Soon neither was he.

Mariella woke up early the next morning and noticed her message light blinking. She took the message off and recognized it was from Todd Fitzgerald, the man who'd discovered her. "Hi Mariella. Sorry this is short notice, but I could really use your help. We want to promote a new project for a difficult client I've just signed with, and having you a part of the project would give us the recognition we need. I'm not sure we can pay you your usual fee, but we'll come up with something. Let me know what you think."

Ian came out of the bedroom. "What are you doing so early?"

"Todd, an old friend of mine, needs me for a modeling job."

"Tell him you're not available."

"I'm not going to turn him down."

Ian stilled. "I thought you weren't going to model any more."

"I'm doing a favor for a friend."

Ian slowly nodded. "I see, and this is just once."

"Yes."

He sat down in front of her. "What if another friend asks you?"

She set her pen down and folded her arms on the table. "Would that be a problem?"

"Depends."

"On what?"

"Whether I'm going to date a model or a photographer."

"Because you don't date models?"

"Exactly."

"Oh, I see," she said slowly, considering each word. "So I'm just a career to you. I'm not a woman."

"I didn't say that."

"You didn't have to. You're giving me an ultimatum. As a photographer I'm welcome in your life, but as a model I'm not. It doesn't matter that I'm the same woman."

"You won't be the same woman. A career defines you. It links you to your past."

"You mean it links me to your father. That's the real problem. You're Ian, the serious one. You date photographers and women of action. It's your father who dates vacuous models and you don't want to have any association with him."

"Photographers don't usually get their names in the tabloids. I want to live my life quietly."

"We've already had our names linked in the papers."

"I know but that will die down soon, but the minute you start modeling again the world feels they own you."

"A few modeling jobs won't change my profile. And this is just one job. I may do a few more down the road. I don't know, but I won't be dictated to or given ultimatums. I'm a grown woman. Now if you want to be in my life you'll have to accept that."

He stood. "I'm not sharing you with the world."

"You're not sharing me with anyone."

"You say that now but you don't mean it. I had to share Jeremiah with the world. I had to share Cathleen with her work. I want someone I can claim as my own. Completely mine. Someone with whom I don't feel like I'm in second place."

"You're not in second place, but I'm not going to turn down a friend just to prove that. You'll have to trust me."

He grabbed his jacket. "I'm sorry. I can't."

She watched him head toward the front door, her heart sinking. "You can't trust me?"

"No, I can't go through this again." He opened the door. "Goodbye."

"Don't."

He turned to her. "What?"

"Every time we argue you walk away and close a door in my face. I hate that."

"Fine." He released the door handle.

"I just need to know one thing."

"What?"

"Were you going to ask me to marry you last night?"

He looked ready to deny it then gave a terse nod.

"I would have said yes." She hugged herself. "Sad, isn't it?"

He took a step toward her. "It doesn't have to be."

"Yes, it does. Because saying 'yes' to you means saying 'no' to part of myself. I can't do that."

He backed away. "I understand."

She shook her head, heartbroken. "No, you don't and that's the saddest part of all."

"Thanks for doing this," Todd said at the end of the shoot.

Mariella only nodded.

Todd watched her, concerned. She'd been professional throughout the shoot. Arriving on time, doing as instructed although Mariella rarely needed any instruction. She was a natural in front of the camera and could exude any mood required of her. But she seemed less vibrant than usual. "Is something wrong?"

"No," she said, gathering her things.

"Because if you're interested in restarting your modeling career I know of an agency…"

She vehemently shook her head. "No, that's not it." She softened her tone. "But thanks."

"Hey, I'm always here for you."

She smiled sadly. "I wish all men were like you."

"If you're having men troubles there's only one cure."

"What?"

"Work."

Mariella took his suggestion to heart. She buried herself in work and traveled. She spent a week in France, then Portugal and flirted with as many men as she could, getting a number of proposals. When she returned to the States she felt renewed. Thoughts of Ian always brought pain, but she was careful not to let them enter her thoughts too frequently. No man would claim her. She was a free woman and that was the way it would always be. She couldn't wait for the gallery opening in less than three days; then she'd never have to deal with Ian Cooper again.

Before reaching home, she stopped in a store close by and bought a few items. Then she saw a picture on the cover of a tabloid that nearly made her scream.

Chapter 19

"You could have stopped him."

Ian stared at his mother across the dinner table. She'd been staying with him the last week since she and Otis were "off again." He wasn't thrilled with her visit or her new companion, a Shih Tzu she called Muffin.

"Gen is a wonderful woman."

"But she used to be a—"

"No one needs to know that and he only told you because he thought you should know."

"I wish he hadn't." She stroked Muffin who slept on her lap. "My only consolation is that you broke off that infatuation you had with that woman."

"Her name is Mariella."

"I know perfectly well what her name is," she snapped. "You don't know how awful it is for a mother to worry about her sons."

"When are you going back to Otis?"

"Maybe never. He still wants to marry me, but he can be so oppressive."

"You have a week."

She stared. "What?"

"I'm only giving you a week to make up your mind."

"But—"

"No. Every spring or summer you argue with Otis and end up here. I'm tired of it. You either decide to marry the man or don't."

"Ian—"

"He's a good man and he loves you and if you can't see that then you don't deserve him and should just surround yourself with little dogs you can dress up and order around."

Shirley stared at him, openmouthed.

Ian threw down his napkin. "Personally, I'm sick of babysitting you and I'm not going to do it anymore. Grow up and support Josh on his choice. God knows you never supported me on anything."

"Ian," Shirley said, hurt by his words. "That's not true."

"Then act like our mother. Not Jeremiah's victim. You have a man and two sons who love you. You're soon going to have a daughter-in-law who will hopefully be blind to your faults and learn to love you as well. Now stop finding reasons to be miserable and start to live your life."

Shirley sat paralyzed, unsure how to respond to her son's tirade. "You've changed."

Ian picked up his napkin and resumed his dinner.

Before she could say more, Josh burst into the room. "I told you that you couldn't trust her."

Ian looked at him. "What are you talking about?"

Josh tossed down a magazine that showed a picture that Mariella had taken of Ian outside the Vermont house smiling up at her. It was splashed on the cover under the headline "Their Private Hideaway." "I'm talking about this."

"Where did they get this photo?" Mariella demanded, pacing her living room.

Gen sat on the couch with her hands clasped in her lap. "I don't know."

"How could this have happened? I kept it hidden."

"Someone must have seen it."

"That's impossible. No one has been in this apartment except Ian and myself and of course you. I just invited the Stantons over one time for dinner…" She stopped.

"What?"

"No, it couldn't be."

"What?"

"Hannah searched the house for a missing earring."

"You don't think she—"

"It's possible. She doesn't like me very much."

"Do you think she would do this?"

"It's possible." She picked up the phone and dialed the Stanton residence. Hannah answered.

"Hello, Hannah, did you see a certain paper today?"

"The one with Mr. Cooper on the cover?"

"Yes."

"Do you know how that picture got there?"

She lowered her voice. "I might. Oops, I hear Mom coming. We can talk later." She hung up.

Mariella gripped the receiver, listening to the dial tone.

"Well?" Gen asked.

Mariella carefully set the receiver down. "Hannah had something to do with it. She wants to talk later." Mariella opened her laptop to book a flight to Georgia. "But I want to talk now."

"I didn't see it as a big deal," Hannah said without remorse. "Personally, I think it's a sexy picture."

"How much did you get for it?"

Hannah shrugged. "I don't remember. Wasn't much. It's not like you're that popular. I mean if you were a real celebrity—"

"That's enough," Gregory said.

Yolanda looked devastated. "Mariella, I'm so sorry."

"Yes, but you're not the one who should be apologizing." She looked at Hannah who boldly stared back. With a secret smirk that said "next time you won't mess with me."

Yolanda sighed. "If there's anything we could do. She'll definitely be punished."

Hannah didn't look concerned by the threat. Mariella resisted the urge to slap the smug look off of her face. She rose to her feet and calmly said, "No, there's nothing. Goodbye."

Mariella had reached her car when someone called her name. She turned and saw Tatiana. "I'm so sorry. Hannah can be such a bitch. I heard her tell a friend that she was going to get you back, but I didn't think—"

"It's okay, it's not your fault."

"But it is my fault. I'm so stupid."

Mariella stilled. "Why?"

"Because I took the picture. Hannah has a habit of going through people's drawers and I saw her in your room and told her to leave and she did. Then I saw the picture in the drawer and I saw it was curling at the end and I thought it would be nice to frame it for you. It was going to be a surprise. So I made a copy and returned it after we went shopping." She lowered her head miserably. "This is all my fault."

"No," Mariella said with a sad smile. "It was my fault." She turned and opened her car door. "I shouldn't have taken his picture in the first place."

Back in New York Mariella stared at the phone. Twice she'd picked it up and put it down again. She wanted to explain, she wanted to defend herself, but she knew there was nothing she could do after destroying his trust. When the phone rang she jumped then checked the number and answered.

"What's going on?" Isabella asked.

Mariella told her everything, tears streaming down her face.

"Have you told him?"

"No."

"Call him."

"I can't," she said in a small voice.

Isabella paused then said, "What are you afraid of?"

She closed her eyes against tears and bit her lip until she felt the salty taste of blood on her tongue.

"Mariella?"

"I'm useless," she whispered, gripping the phone until her knuckles paled.

"No, you're not."

"Yes, I am. I'm nothing better than a finely sculptured statue. Nice to look at but useless. You know that's true. When Dad was dying he called for you."

"Mariella, he just wanted something to drink. He didn't know he'd die."

"When Mom was dying she called for you."

"I was like her nurse."

"The last week of Jeremiah's life he wouldn't let me see him. He didn't want me around. And then he..."

"Mariella, that didn't mean they didn't love you."

"No, but they didn't *need* me. I was useless to them. I loved them, but there was nothing I could do. I felt helpless and I hate feeling helpless and I feel helpless now. No one has ever needed me and Ian certainly doesn't. He was able to walk away from me without looking back. And now he has the perfect reason to prove that his decision was right. *I* caused this problem and there's nothing I can do to fix it. The picture is out there for everyone to see. I betrayed his trust and he must hate me now more than I hate myself."

"You don't know if you won't talk to him."

"I can't face the rejection. I can't give him the power to reject me."

"But if you don't take the risk, you may be losing something precious."

"I've already lost it." She dabbed her lip with a napkin. "I love him. He has my heart and he can destroy me. He has a power over me that I hate admitting."

"Loving someone isn't like being a loser in a battle."

"It is to me. I like being in control. I like being the strong one. I don't like being vulnerable to anyone. You don't understand, Isabella. Men don't fall in love with women like me. Not really. We're fun for a time and nice to look at and nice to own, but they don't love us. Not the way Alex loves you."

"Mariella, when you two were here I saw how he looked at you. I think he cares about you more than you think."

"No, the moment I started modeling again he left." She wiped her tears away, gathering courage. "I'm going to fight this and I'm going to forget him. I'm sorry this happened, but I won't apologize."

"What about the gallery showing?"

"I'll arrive late and leave early. He'll ignore me. That's his way of teaching me a lesson."

"I still think you should call him. He might not have supported your modeling, but he does deserve an explanation. I know you hate that, but it's time to grow up. You make mistakes, you have to admit them."

Shirley stared at the closed door of Ian's darkroom. He'd been in there for hours. She knew it was his hideaway and was sorry that he felt the need to hide from her. If there was one thing she could teach him it was how to deal with betrayal and heartache. But she wondered if one could ever fix a broken heart.

Her divorce had left her bitter and made it difficult to believe in love. It was even harder to believe in it when one had been married to an egotistical womanizer with a God complex. Shirley Cooper knew Otis was nothing like Jeremiah. Otis didn't have Jeremiah's wandering eye or his brilliance and Otis was rich and she wanted to enjoy the life she'd become accustomed to. But she feared once they were married he'd lose interest in her. She couldn't compete with younger women and damn it, after sixty-some years and two kids she shouldn't have to. She wasn't afraid of growing older. She was afraid of trusting again. Of letting herself become vulnerable again. Her judgment had been so poor before and she didn't want to make that mistake again and she didn't want to see Ian make that mistake either.

She slept soundly that night, then woke up to the sound of roaring engines. She opened her balcony window and saw Otis climbing down from a helicopter ladder.

"What are you doing?"

"Shirley, I need to talk to you."

"You could get killed."

"Doesn't matter. I'm dying without you by my side."

"Don't be silly."

He signaled to the helicopter. Rose petals fell around them. "I can't fix your past, but I can promise you a future filled with my love. I love you, Shirley, and I want you to be my wife."

"I'm frightened."

"Honey, I'm frightened now, but I'm willing to take the risk because I love you so much."

"I love you too. Now get down from there so I can show you my answer."

"It'd better be a yes."

"I promise it will be much, much more."

"How much do you think she got for it?" Josh asked as he and Ian sat in his office. Although Ian had told him about their mother's upcoming nuptials yesterday's story still occupied Josh's thoughts.

"I don't care," Ian said. Of course that was a lie. He was trying not to remember the sight of Mariella teasing him in the woods of Vermont and promising him that no one would see the picture. And he felt stupid that he had believed her.

"I told you not to trust her."

"I know."

"So what are you going to do?"

"First I'm going to hand the magazine over to you, then I'm going to take my camera into the most dangerous war zone I can find and try to get myself shot."

Josh stared at him, appalled. "What?"

"Then perhaps I can get away from you telling me 'I told you so' every ten minutes."

Josh frowned. "That's not funny."

"I'm not trying to be funny."

"You have to do something."

Ian shrugged. "I'm trying to work, but you keep talking."

Josh looked around for someone to share his frustration, but only saw Sylvester and Candy. Then someone knocked.

"Come in," Ian said.

Nelson came into the room, but before he could speak Josh pounced on him. "Ah, Nelson, just the man I need."

Nelson sent him a weary glance. "Yes?"

"What do you think about that picture and story of my brother in the paper?"

Nelson glanced at Ian then back at Josh and nervously cleared his throat. "I don't think anything."

"Come on, you can be honest—it won't cost you your job."

"I'd really prefer not to say anything."

Serita came up behind Nelson. "Um, Mr. Cooper."

Josh looked at her with hope. "Serita, you can be honest with me. What did you think of the story about my brother and the picture?"

"I didn't think anything."

His face fell. "What?"

"They got the story wrong and besides, it's just a picture."

Ian stared at her as though she'd just unraveled a mystery. "It's just a picture?" he echoed.

"Yes."

"Yes," Ian said. Suddenly everything clicked: Jeremiah, the magazine, the will—it all made sense. He finally saw what his father wanted him to see all along. Images were only as powerful as you made them; life wasn't black and white.

Serita sent Josh a worried look. "Are you okay, Mr. Cooper?"

He slapped his forehead. "I've been an idiot." He jumped to his feet. "I have to get started."

"On what?"

"My plan."

"But what about Mariella?"

"Don't worry, when Mariella shows up at the gallery I'll be ready for her."

"You think she'll come?"

"I know she will."

Chapter 20

The night of the gallery opening was a success. Everyone who was of any importance in New York was at the opening. Most of the women were adorned in expensive jewelry and gowns, and the men either in black tie or smartly fitted Italian suits. When Mariella entered all eyes were on her. She was dressed in a ruffled designer gown that accentuated her figure. Her hair was in flat double-twist, swept upwards and held in place with an emerald-and-pearl hair comb.

Mariella was aware of the eyes following her, but waited for the gaze of only one man. She walked through the exhibit, impressed with what

Ian had done. The gallery space was large and open, with photographs displayed in see-through plastic frames suspended from the ceiling. A labyrinth of freestanding walls created a maze through which guests walked looking at enormous blowups of photos, juxtaposed against floor-to-ceiling colorful abstract sculptures.

"I've never seen anything like this," someone said.

"It's marvelous," another replied.

Mariella accepted a champagne glass and silently toasted Jeremiah. She knew he would be proud. But the comments and congratulatory shakes meant nothing to her. There was only one person she wanted to see. She wanted a chance to explain. She needed one.

When she finally saw Ian across the room she froze, but when he looked right at her without any recognition she could feel herself wither inside. She finished the contents of her champagne, gathering courage. No matter how he looked at her, she would tell him the truth. He deserved that much. She gave the glass to a passing waiter then headed toward him.

"It's wonderful!" Isabella said, seizing her arm.

"She's been saying that nonstop," Alex said.

Mariella hugged them. "I'm glad you two could make it."

"And I'm glad that you and Ian patched things up."

Mariella frowned. "What are you talking about?"

"The wing dedicated to all your photographs."

"That's just part of Jeremiah's project."

"No, it isn't. Come on." Isabella grabbed her sister's hand and led her to a separate area crowded with visitors. In large letters it read: The Mariella Duvall Collection. Ian had taken her "extra" pictures, the ones he had refused to include in the project, the pictures of Teresa in Georgia, the sunsets in Vermont and others.

"I don't understand," Mariella said breathlessly.

"Neither do I," Josh said from behind them, "But Ian insisted. He said he wanted to give you what you wanted."

Mariella turned and raced out of the room. She weaved her way through the crush of people hoping to spot Ian, where she'd last seen him. But he was nowhere to be found. Tears of frustration gathered in her eyes. Everyone else thought tonight was a triumph, she'd completed the last works of Jeremiah Cooper and had her first gallery showing, but she saw it as a mockery. All that she had hoped and dreamed for seemed empty without the one person she wanted to share it with.

She retrieved her coat and left. She was tired of pretending to smile; tired of pretending she didn't care. She was tired of *pretending* full stop. She pushed open the front glass doors and stormed down the stairs wanting to punch Ian in the nose and say: *Why did you do this to me? Why did you have to make me care until it hurt? Why? Why did you make loving you one of the worst decisions of my life?*

"That's not very nice," a deep voice said above her.

Mariella spun around and saw Ian standing at the top of the stairs. It had been so long since she'd last seen him she wasn't sure it was him at first. Something about him had changed. He still wore black and she could hardly distinguish him from the night sky. He still had a low voice that could rip through silence and eyes that burned with intensity. And yet…there was something different about him. Mariella gripped the handle of her purse knowing there was no use trying to analyze a man she would never understand. "What's not nice?"

He walked toward her. "You shouldn't leave so soon."

She swallowed, her heart racing, making breathing difficult, but she did not move. "There's no reason to stay."

He stopped a step above her. "I thought I'd created plenty of reason. Didn't you like my surprise?"

"No."

He looked startled. "No?" He gestured to the building. "I thought this is what you wanted."

"Then you don't know me very well. You're not even angry."

"Why should I be angry?"

"Because of the picture in the paper."

"Mariella—"

"At least if you were angry with me I'd know you cared. Instead you're punishing me by pretending that nothing happened, that I hadn't betrayed your trust. You're treating me like… like someone who doesn't matter to you. That what we shared was nothing." Her voice trembled and tears stung her eyes. "And I'm not going to cry because I won't let you make me cry." She angrily wiped away a tear. "You wanted to hurt me and it's working. I only came here today to tell you how sorry I am and ask your forgiveness."

"Mariella—"

"And I hate asking for forgiveness. Especially when I'm so angry at you. How dare you tell me what to do. I'm a woman with an independent mind, but I'm also a woman who loves you, but since that's not enough I hope I never see you again." She turned and headed down the rest of the stairs.

Ian jumped in front of her. "I made a mistake."

She halted. "What?"

"You're right. I shouldn't have told you what to do with your life because of my own…" He shook his head, not finding the right word. "I didn't like the thought of sharing you with the world. Of seeing your face all over the place, of women admiring you and men lusting after you. I didn't like that you would be out there exposed to attack that I couldn't protect you from. But I realized I'd rather deal with that than lose you. That picture you took of me made me realize that no matter how many people saw it, that moment was still ours. Others can interpret it the way they want to but only we know the truth. I was arrogant and wrong to make you choose me over your career. I don't care what you do as long as you'll say you'll be mine."

His eyes clung to hers, but it wasn't their expression that captured her attention. It wasn't even his words. It was his face: open, real, hopeful. That was what had changed him, he now had hope. The man standing before her was no longer a mystery; his dark shadows had disappeared. A happiness so pure and full spread through her and she was no longer afraid of loving him, it felt like a gift.

Mariella cupped the side of his face, knowing that she would never tire of gazing at him. "I always promised myself I'd never let a man own me."

A slow smile touched Ian's lips. "Nobody could own you any more than they could own me." He slid his arm around her waist and drew her close. "But I'd like to borrow you for the next fifty years if you don't mind."

Mariella wrapped her arms around his neck. "I think I could arrange that."

"Then let's come to an agreement." He lowered his head and kissed her with all the passion of a man claiming a well-earned prize.

Stunned silence followed when Ian and Mariella returned to the gallery and announced their engagement. After a long awkward moment the crowd gave a muted, but polite, applause.

Only Isabella showed her enthusiasm by throwing her arms around her sister and spinning her around then hugging Ian until Alex had to pull her away. Gen wasn't sure about the match, but was glad to see her friend happy and told her so. They were soon surrounded by a crowd of well-wishers, but after a few moments Mariella disappeared from Ian's side and soon the crowds thinned again and turned their attention back to the showing.

Otis came up to Ian and shook his hand. "Congratulations, or should I say good luck? From what your mother told me you have a wild one on your hands."

Ian shook his head. "She's a perfect lamb."

"I can't believe you can say that with a straight face," Josh said, joining the two men. "She'll run the house."

"And she'll run him," Otis said.

"I know that my brother loves a challenge, but Mariella will prove to be a challenge beyond even him."

"I disagree," Ian said. "I'm marrying the gentlest, most tenderhearted woman in the room."

Both men burst into laughter. "You can't be serious," Josh said. "Everyone knows how miserable your fiancée is." He swept his hand through the air. "I can see the headline now: 'Innocent Ian Marries Mad Mariella.'"

"They won't be calling her that anymore."

"You intend to stop them?" Otis asked.

"No, they won't have a reason to."

Josh sniffed. "There will always be a reason with Mariella around."

"And again I disagree," Ian said. "To prove my point let us each call our fiancées and ask them to leave early. The first woman to reply immediately wins the wager."

"You think that Mariella will leave all this admiration because you ask her to? No, brother, you're going to embarrass yourself."

Ian shrugged. "You don't wish to bet?"

"I'll bet you a hundred," Otis said.

Josh nodded. "Yes, a hundred."

"And I wager you a thousand that Mariella will come at my first call."

Otis laughed again. "Okay then. Who's first?"

"I am," Josh said. He signaled to a waiter who'd served them earlier in the evening. "Please go and tell Ms. Gen Moser that we are leaving early."

The waiter soon disappeared, but just as quickly returned. "She says that she wants a few more minutes."

Ian raised a sly brow. "Oh dear, is she too busy to answer your request?"

"Don't brag, brother," Josh grumbled. "Mariella will give you a worse answer."

Otis touched the waiter's shoulder. "Go and tell Mrs. Shirley Cooper that I want to talk to her."

"How will I know her?"

"She has a Shih Tzu hanging out of her purse," Ian said.

Otis glared at him. "And she's wearing a blue dress."

"So is the dog."

The waiter hid a smile and left then soon returned with his shoulders slumped. "She said that she will not come and that if you have anything to say that you should go to her."

Ian raised both his brows. "Yes, a very biddable fiancée indeed."

Otis raised his chin. "I doubt yours will even give you a response."

Ian looked at the waiter. "Please tell Ms. Mariella Duvall that it's time to go."

The waiter hesitated. "Now?"

"Yes. Now."

He tugged on his collar then left. Before Otis and Josh could tease Ian for the waiter's long absence they spotted a striking figure making her way through the crowd.

"It can't be," Josh said.

But it was. Mariella stopped in front of Ian and said, "You're ready to go?"

"Yes."

"Just let me get my jacket."

Josh stared at her in amazement, then caught sight of Gen. "You just cost me money."

She looked at him blankly. "Why?"

"He lost a bet," Ian said.

"It was silly of you to make a wager."

Shirley approached the group. "What did you want?"

Otis gloomily shook his head. "It doesn't matter now."

"They were betting on us," Gen said.

Shirley shrugged. "Men will always be boys. Why would I obey a man's command?"

"No woman should obey *any* man's command," Mariella said. "However, a man who has pledged his life to protect me and provide for me and love me until the day of his last breath." She looked at Ian. "For *that* man I will come when called. I will listen when spoken to and I will answer when asked. I welcome being his companion, helpmate, lover and friend. I would walk on hot fires for him, because we are of one heart and one spirit and whatever he would ask me to do, he would do himself. Am I right?"

Ian smiled. "Absolutely."

Everyone stared at Mariella in shock. Ian took her hand. "Before we go I want to show you something." He gestured to the announcer.

The announcer then said, "Everyone please gather in the Duvall wing where her most important piece will be revealed."

Under a buzz of murmurs the crowd walked into the last exhibit room where a large covered canvas hung. Ian nodded to an attendant who removed the covering and revealed the image of Ian that had been splattered all over the tabloids.

Mariella gasped. "What have you done?"

"I'm displaying your work." He nodded to the picture. "This is one of your best and I want everyone to see it."

She folded her arms and sent him a sly glance. "Because it's a picture of you?"

"No." He stood behind her and wrapped his arms around her waist and whispered, "Because it's a picture of a man smiling at the woman he loves."

*A dramatic new novel about learning
to trust again...*

Essence **bestselling author**

ANITA BUNKLEY

SUITE
Embrace

Too many Mr. Wrongs has made Skylar Webster gun-shy.
But seductive Olympic athlete Mark Jorgen is awfully
tempting. Mark's tempted, too, enough to consider
changing his globe-trotting, playboy ways. But first he'll
have to earn Skylar's trust.

"Anita Bunkley has a gift for bringing wonderful ethnic
characters and their unique problems to readers in a
dramatic, sweeping novel of tragedy and triumph."
—*Romantic Times BOOKreviews* on *Wild Embers*

Coming the first week of January wherever books are sold.

KIMANI™
ROMANCE

www.kimanipress.com

KPAB0480108

To love thy brother...

National bestselling author

Robyn Amos

Lilah's LIST

Dating R&B megastar Reggie Martin was #1 on
Lilah Banks's top-ten list of things to accomplish before
turning thirty. But Reggie's older brother Tyler is making
a wish list of his own—and seducing Lilah into falling
in love with him is *his* #1.

"Robyn Amos has once again created a sensational couple
that draws us into a whirlpool of sensuality, suspense and
romance, while continuing to make her talent for writing
bestselling novels seem effortless."
—*Romantic Times BOOKreviews* on *True Blue*

Coming the first week of January wherever books are sold.

KIMANI™
ROMANCE

www.kimanipress.com   KPRA0490108

A deliciously sensual tale of passion and revenge…

Sweeter *Than* Revenge

Bestselling author

Ann CHRISTOPHER

When daddy cuts her off, Maria must take a position as executive assistant to David Hunt—a man who once broke her heart. But David's back in her life for only one reason— revenge! And he knows the sweetest way to get it.…

Coming the first week of January wherever books are sold.

KIMANI™
ROMANCE

www.kimanipress.com

KPAC0510108

*Even a once-in-a-lifetime love
deserves a second chance.*

USA TODAY Bestselling Author

BRENDA
JACKSON

WHISPERED PROMISES

A Madaris Family novel.

When Caitlin Parker is called to her father's deathbed,
she's shocked to find her ex-husband, Dex Madaris,
there, as well. It's been four years since Caitlin and Dex
said goodbye, shattering the promise of an everlasting
love that never was. But the true motive for their
unexpected reunion soon comes to light, as does the
daughter Dex never knew existed—a secret Caitlin
fears Dex will never forgive....

"Brenda Jackson has written another sensational novel…
stormy, sensual and sexy—all the things a romance reader
could want in a love story."
—*Romantic Times BOOKreviews* on *Whispered Promises*

**Available the first week of January
wherever books are sold.**

ARABESQUE®

www.kimanipress.com

KPBJ0510108

Featuring the voices of eighteen of your
favorite authors…

ON THE LINE

Essence Bestselling Author

donna hill

A sexy, irresistible story starring Joy Newhouse,
who, as a radio relationship expert, is considered
the diva of the airwaves. But when she's fired,
Joy quickly discovers that if she can dish it out,
she'd better be able to take it!

Featuring contributions by such favorite authors
as Gwynne Forster, Monica Jackson, Earl Sewell,
Phillip Thomas Duck and more!

Coming the first week of January,
wherever books are sold.

sepia™

www.kimanipress.com   KPDH0211207